WHEN LOVE IS LOST

It is 1948 . . . Louisa Barton is beginning a new life as a school-teacher, after the disappearance of her husband, Michael, who, though surviving the War unscathed, went missing soon afterwards in mysterious circumstances. At the school, Louisa befriends Susannah, a new first-year pupil, who has her own air of mystery. But Louisa's new found peace is soon shattered when a stranger turns up on her doorstep one dark night . . .

Books by Marlene E. McFadden
in the Linford Romance Library:

PATH OF TRUE LOVE
TOMORROW ALWAYS COMES

MARLENE E. McFADDEN

WHEN LOVE
IS LOST

Complete and Unabridged

LINFORD
Leicester

First published in Great Britain in 2004

First Linford Edition
published 2005

British Library CIP Data

McFadden, Marlene E. (Marlene Elizabeth), *1937 –*
When love is lost.—Large print ed.—
Linford romance library
1. Love stories
2. Large type books
I. Title
823.9′14 [F]

ISBN 1–84395–825–2

Published by
F. A. Thorpe (Publishing)
Anstey, Leicestershire
Set by Words & Graphics Ltd.
Anstey, Leicestershire
Printed and bound in Great Britain by
T. J. International Ltd., Padstow, Cornwall

This book is printed on acid-free paper

1

Louisa Barton looked down at the sea of faces below her. Rows upon rows of girls dressed in navy blue skirts or gymslips, depending on their age, white blouses and dark red school ties, most singing with gusto the traditional beginning of term hymn.

Only the first couple of rows were not as sure of the words — the new girls, the first-timers, most looking slightly bewildered, the lucky ones, some might say, who had managed to pass their eleven-plus exams.

Louisa could understand their feelings of nervousness and apprehension. Didn't she feel like that herself? This was her first term, too, at Langley Hall Secondary School. She was exactly the same, except she was twenty-eight and they were only eleven. But she like them would have to get used to strange

1

faces and to digest new rules and regulations.

It was September 7, 1948, and Louisa was beginning her new job as teacher of English at the school. It was to be a fresh phase in her life, a fresh start; a time to look forward, to learn to live again and to accept that Michael was never coming home.

It had taken her a long time to accept that. Even the War Office's cold, official statement hadn't convinced her. How could it? They couldn't possibly know that Michael was dead. No-one could. How had he died? Where had he died? Why was his body never found?

He had returned almost unscathed from Europe in 1945, his only injuries two broken ribs from playing rugby. He had arrived at the disembarkation camp in Reading and had then been moved to the Dispersal Unit at Northampton. He had written her a letter from there, telling her how much he missed her, giving an amusing description of the awful brown demob suit he had been given as a leaving present.

And then, nothing. It was as though he had walked out of the camp and simply disappeared off the face of the earth. An enquiry had been set up, searches made but all to no avail. No-one could say where Michael was. And the worst part of all was when she was told that after seven years, she would be able to officially declare her husband, Michael John Barton, dead.

To enable her to get on with her life, to push herself into a new direction by going to teacher's training college, working hard, passing examinations with credit, Louisa had to tell herself that Michael was dead. She had to grieve for him and start to remember the good times, the love they had shared. She had to face life without him.

It hadn't been easy, but standing on the platform of the gymnasium which also served as an assembly hall, with the other teachers alongside her, Louisa felt she had made it. She had hope, in the future and in herself.

The hymn came to an end. Children coughed, feet shuffled. Miss Cayton, the headmistress, came to the edge of the platform.

'Let us pray,' she intoned.

All heads bowed, Louisa's amongst them.

'Our Father, who art in Heaven . . . ' The headmistress lead the whole school into the familiar words of the Lord's Prayer.

Louisa found herself praying, 'Dear God, please look after Michael, wherever he is.'

When Louisa started to pack her books at the end of the school day she had to admit it hadn't gone badly and she felt she had established rapport with the girls from Form 1B, which was to be her class for the next school year. The girls all seemed bright and eager to learn.

The school seemed quiet, empty, as by now most of the girls would have left and Louisa was surprised when she

4

heard footsteps coming along the corridor outside the classroom. It wasn't a pupil. Every girl at Langley Hall had to wear gym shoes indoors to protect the polished, wooden floors from clomping, heavy shoes. Only the teachers were exempt from this rule and the footsteps seemed quite loud.

Miss Cayton appeared in the open doorway.

'Ah, Mrs Barton,' she said with a smile, 'I'm glad you're still here. I just wanted to find out how your day went.'

'Very well, thank you, Miss Cayton,' Louisa said.

'Good.' The headmistress came farther into the room.

She was a tall, angular woman, perhaps in her late forties, with dark brown short hair and kind eyes. She carried herself well and wore her black gown proudly. As Louisa understood it, no other teacher wore a gown except at speech days and other official functions.

'I wanted you to know,' Miss Cayton went on, 'that I am so pleased you've joined the staff of Langley Hall. I think you'll be a real asset.' She paused, came and sat on the corner of the desk, and looked down at her hands. 'Of course I am fully aware of your ... er ... personal tragedy.'

Louisa felt herself stiffening. How did she know? This hadn't been mentioned by Louisa at her interview with Miss Cayton, though she had made the education authorities aware of her circumstances.

Miss Cayton put her hand gently on Louisa's shoulder.

'Don't worry, my dear, no-one else will get to know unless you wish it. I will just say now, how sorry I am and leave it at that.'

Louisa's head jerked up proudly.

'I won't let anything interfere with my duties here, Miss Cayton,' she declared.

'Of course you won't. I never thought that you would.' She stood up straight again. 'And now, what do you think of your girls, eh?'

Her smile was quite mischievous.

Louisa relaxed, sorry she had reacted the way she had. The headmistress meant well and was only trying to be kind. It was understandable that she, as head of Langley Hall, would be told the background of any teacher under her authority.

'I like them,' she declared, 'and I think they like me.'

'We have some very nice girls here,' Miss Cayton agreed. 'Of course, I don't suppose there's any school that doesn't have a smattering of problem children.'

'There was just one child. Oh, she's not a problem, I'm not saying that, she's very sweet actually. Quite beautiful, especially her eyes, but she seems so . . . well . . . thin, undernourished perhaps, nervous and jumpy and in a way, scared. Oh, perhaps I'm making too much of it . . . ' Louisa broke off, feeling awkward.

'Are you talking about Susannah Priestley?' Miss Cayton asked gently.

'Why, yes.'

7

'Susannah's is a sad story. She's an adopted child and her adoptive parents were into middle age when she went to them. Then two years ago Mrs Priestley died in a tragic accident, crushed to death under the wheels of a tractor driven by her husband on their family farm. Mr Priestley was, naturally, totally devastated.'

'How awful!' Louisa breathed.

Miss Cayton went on, 'After the accident, Susannah's father seemed to go to pieces. He began to resent her, reject her and he also started drinking. Oh, he's not a habitual drunkard, nothing like that, but he simply lost the will and the ability to cope. I know all this from Mr Priestley himself. He came along to the parents' interview that I insist on for all new starters. Of course, it's usually the mothers who talk candidly to me about their daughters, but Jack Priestley didn't have that option, and I'm glad he felt able to confide in me. He does his best, poor man, but I wanted you to know about Susannah and it's all to your credit, Louisa, if may called you Louisa, that you have been so perceptive about her.'

'Thank you,' Louisa said, feeling so sorry for the child and hoping she would be able to encourage her.

'Susannah is a somewhat lonely child, with no particular friends and I feel she may find it difficult to make special friends here either.'

'I'll do my best to help her, Miss Cayton,' Louisa promised.

The headmistress smiled.

'I know I can rely on you,' she said. 'Now, I'd better let you get along home. You'll be taking the path through the woods, I suppose, considering where you live.'

'Yes, I came that way this morning. It's lovely.'

They parted outside the classroom and went their separate ways. Louisa collected her coat from the staff room, thinking about Susannah. On that first day, she had not really been able to assess what the girls' work would be like, but tomorrow she would set an essay for the class, something simple. Outside the school building she saw the headmistress getting into a small dark car and starting off down the long, twisting drive that led to a main road. Louisa herself took the route across the netball pitch towards the path through the dense woods, which would eventually bring her to the rural area quaintly called Squirrel Grove, where she lived with her mother.

Langley Hall was once a private dwelling of a mill owner in the town of Midthorpe, surrounded by fields, woods and a municipal golf course. The hall itself was a magnificent building, the former stables of which now housed the school's gymnasium and science block.

Louisa felt privileged to be teaching at such a school. Midthorpe itself was a large, industrial town with many factories and woollen mills but at the same time it was surrounded by some wild and beautiful Yorkshire countryside. Louisa had been born in Midthorpe and could not ever see herself wanting to live anywhere else.

When she and Michael married, they had rented a tiny, one-bedroomed cottage with no bathroom, but they had loved it. However, when Louisa's father was killed in action in 1943, she had moved back home to be with her mother and now Louisa was glad she had done this, because both she and her mother had lost the men they loved. They got on well together and in many ways were very fortunate in life.

Louisa's mother owned the house, a large, pleasant detached with a nice garden, and she, too, had a job, working from home as a dressmaker, so money was not a problem. They also grew their own vegetables and were what could be called comfortably-off.

The woods were quiet, except for Louisa's footsteps and she felt at ease with herself, pleased by how the day had gone, looking forward to telling her mother all about it. She approached a wide bend in the path and pulled up short when she saw a group of girls ahead of her. It was plain they had neither seen nor heard her.

There were four girls pulling and tugging on the arms of a much smaller girl. Louisa saw at once that this girl was Susannah Priestley. She started to move forward, ready to call out, when Susannah, with some determination, managed to drag herself free. Instead of running away, she stood and faced her tormentors.

'You're not going to throw me into no holly bush,' she yelled. 'I'm wearing me new uniform. Me dad'll kill me if I get it dirty or torn.'

One of the other girls yelled back, 'You're a new girl, you've got to be initiated. New girls always are.'

'Not me!' Susannah retorted, standing there, her fists clenched, her thin legs firmly planted. 'If you touch me again I'll scratch your eyes out. I'll knock your front teeth out.'

She could only be described as spitting fire and the older girls hesitated, looking at each other, unsure of what to do next.

Then one of them, a tall red haired girl with freckles saw Louisa.

'It's Mrs Barton,' she hissed.

Louisa marched forward and the culprits stood looking down.

'What's going on here?' she demanded in her most imperious voice.

'Nothing, Mrs Barton,' the red-haired girl mumbled.

Louisa turned to Susannah. 'Well, Susannah?' she asked gently.

Susannah turned her dark eyes on Louisa.

'Nothing, Mrs Barton,' she said.

'Then, off you go. Do you live this way?'

'Yes, at Ivy Farm.'

Louisa didn't know exactly where Ivy Farm was but there was open countryside beyond Squirrel Grove so she supposed it was somewhere in that direction which must be quite a walk for Susannah every day.

Susannah rushed away, soon disappearing and Louisa faced the downcast girls.

'I want your names and your form number,' she said.

One by one, looking thoroughly miserable, the girls gave the information Louisa asked for.

'You can count yourselves fortunate that I'm not going to report this matter to Miss Cayton,' she told them icily. 'Bullying will not be tolerated at Langley Hall. Do you understand me?'

'Yes, Mrs Barton,' they chorused as one.

'Good. And if I ever catch you doing something like this again you'll be in big trouble. Now get off home.'

They needed no second bidding.

Left alone, Louisa permitted herself a small smile. Good for Susannah, she thought. She had certainly stood up to the older girls and she must have been frightened. At that particular point the holly bushes were thick and prickly, not a happy prospect to be threatened with being thrown in there. Louisa felt she must re-think her first impression of Susannah. Not quite the little, frightened mouse she had originally seemed!

2

Louisa entered the house by the back door which lead directly into the large, square kitchen. They rarely used the front door. The kitchen was empty but through the window, Louisa could see her mother down at the bottom of the long garden, moving about amongst the vegetable patch, not bending down as though she was picking vegetables but simply moving between the rows, looking out towards the woods beyond the wooden fence that bordered their property, the same woods that surrounded Langley Hall.

What was she looking for? Louisa banged on the window and her mother turned and waved and presently started walking back along the path towards the house.

Eileen Sanderson was forty-nine, a slim, attractive woman with thick dark hair which she wore in a bun at the back of her head. Louisa had always known her mother was artistic. She was an expert seamstress and cushion covers, chair covers, pillowcases and tablecloths bore testimony to her needlework skills. But her talents didn't stop there. She cooked and baked and turned ration ingredients into sumptuous meals.

The house was beautifully kept. One bedroom had been turned into a dressmaking workshop where Eileen took her many customers for measuring and fitting and then worked wonders on her sewing machine with materials for which they had scrimped and saved. Of course, many of Eileen's customers were quite well-to-do and were pleased to spread her fame amongst their friends by word of mouth.

She came into the kitchen, looking slightly worried.

'Something wrong?' Louisa asked. 'What were you looking at?'

'Not at, for,' Eileen corrected. 'There's

been a man hanging around.'

'A man?' Louisa repeated. 'What sort of a man?'

'A scruffy sort. Badly dressed, dirty, with a beard and long hair.'

'A tramp perhaps?'

'No, I don't think so. There seem to be more about since the war, but they come to the house, quite openly. And they're polite and grateful.'

'And this man was rude?' Louisa asked.

'I never spoke to him, Louisa. I merely saw him, first walking along the edge of the wood and then actually standing on the other side of the fence. The first time I saw him it didn't bother me, then when he came back I started to go out there, to ask him what he wanted, but by the time I got downstairs, he had disappeared.'

'Oh, I'm sure he meant no harm,' Louisa said.

'No, probably not.' Eileen seemed to relax. 'Well, how did it go?'

'Very well.'

'Tell me all about it,' Eileen offered, 'whilst I start supper.'

'Let me get changed first.'

By the time Louisa had changed and gone downstairs her mother seemed to have forgotten the incident and was happily preparing the evening meal. Louisa wanted to help but knew any offers would be rejected, politely but firmly, so she sat at the kitchen table, and talked about her day.

When she came to the incident in the woods Eileen laughed.

'Bullies at a posh girls' school? Shocking!' she cried.

'Langley Hall isn't posh, Mum. It's a state-run school, not a private one. Just ordinary children who have passed their eleven plus that's all. If you're talking posh schools what about Greenfield?'

She smiled when she said this because Greenfield was Eileen's old grammar school and well known to have its fair share of snobs amongst its pupils both present and past.

'Point taken,' Eileen said. 'So you

think you'll like being a teacher?'

'I shall love it. But then, I always knew that I would.'

'Perhaps you should have gone in for it sooner and not waited so long.'

'Michael didn't want me to work, you know that,' she said softly.

Eileen came and sat by Louisa at the table, taking hold of her daughter's hand and giving it a squeeze.

'I'm sorry,' she began. 'I didn't mean to upset you.'

'We must talk about Michael, just as we have to talk about Dad.'

'Yes, I know. You're right. And things can only get easier, can't they?'

'So they say.'

But Louisa knew that now Michael, and her father, too, were very much in both their minds, and after supper they retired to the sitting-room, enjoying an evening glass of sherry and talked quietly about their shared memories. On the mantelpiece was a collection of photographs — one of Louisa's father in his captain's uniform, taken a few months before he was killed; a wedding picture of Louisa and Michael; they had been able to have a white wedding in church on that spring day in 1939 whilst the coming conflict was only a vague and distant threat; a picture of Michael, also in army uniform with his cap perched on the side of his head and a grin on his face. He was so good-looking, dark hair and eyes, charming and funny.

Then there was a photograph of Eileen's brother, Colin, who had died of some mystery virus at the age of twenty-two. Louisa had been fifteen or sixteen at the time and hadn't really known Uncle Colin as Eileen had moved away from her family home, coming to Midthorpe when she married Richard Sanderson. But she did know that her mother had been devoted to her much younger brother, and she had been devastated when he died, though had always been very reluctant to actually talk about the way he did die.

So, tonight, Colin's name, too, was present in their reminiscences. The family photograph albums were produced, and some of the poems that Colin had written as a teenager. They were good, too, and, yes, before the evening was out, a few tears had been shed.

At one point Louisa said, 'If only I knew exactly what happened to Michael. If only, like Dad, he had been killed in action, do you think I might have found that easier to bear?'

'Perhaps. Perhaps not,' Eileen said after a few moments of silence. 'Because a killed-in-action telegram is so utterly final, whilst you . . . ' She seemed to be at a loss to finish her sentence.

'On the other hand, Mum,' Louisa began, 'you know where Dad died, you know where he is buried. My head tells me I must accept that Michael is gone for ever, but my heart . . . it isn't hope, I wouldn't call it hope, more a feeling of frustration of something unfinished in my life.'

They were getting maudlin and suddenly Eileen jumped up and switched on the wireless.

'Let's have a bit of music,' she declared, 'and another glass of sherry.'

The albums were put away and though their departed loved ones seemed to smile down on them from the mantelpiece, Louisa felt she could now relax and was sure her mother could, too. Louisa's mind was now dwelling on the subject for the essay she was planning for Form 1B the next day.

Louisa found time in the afternoon break to look casually at the essays she was planning to read thoroughly and mark that evening, but when she came across Susannah Priestley's exercise book, she put the others on one side to concentrate fully on that. She remembered how, immediately she had written the title she wanted them to use on the blackboard, Susannah had opened her book, picked up her pen and started to scribble fast and furiously, scarcely pausing for breath.

Louisa had found herself sitting staring at the top of the girl's glossy dark head. Around her, the other girls gave away, by their various expressions, some bored, some frustrated, by the chewing of pens and the gazing out of the window, that most of them were finding it difficult composing an essay off the top of their heads.

Now Louisa was deep into Susannah's fascinating story when someone behind her said, 'Looks interesting.'

Louisa looked up to see Christine Yardley, the Art and Drama teacher smiling down at her. Christine was about Louisa's age and they had taken to one another instantly.

Now Louisa said, 'I'm reading Susannah Priestley's essay. Well, it's more than an essay, it's a work of fiction, a short story. So well written. I selected a title at random, The Black Sheep. Don't ask me why, and at a first cursory glance Susannah seems to be the only one who hasn't written about an animal in a field!'

Christine poured herself a cup of tea from the pot on the table by the wall and came to sit by Louisa. Apart from Miss St Clair, the French mistress, the oldest teacher at Langley Hall by all accounts, who appeared to have nodded off in her chair, they were alone in the staff room at that moment.

'It doesn't surprise me, what you say about Susannah,' Christine said, 'I took her for art yesterday and her talent is quite phenomenal.'

'Are you aware of Susannah's background?' Louisa asked.

Christine nodded. 'Oh, yes, Miss Cayton had a special staff meeting during the summer holidays. I take it she told you?'

'Yesterday. Poor child.'

Christine shrugged, 'Well, everyone has their problems, I suppose, and I have a niggly feeling that singling Susannah out in that way might do her more harm than good. I, for one, don't want to be constantly making allowances for her.' She laughed. 'Though if yesterday's work is anything to go by I don't think I shall have to.'

Louisa thought of telling Christine about the incident in the woods, but decided against it. That was an episode she must keep to herself. So, of course, she couldn't mention either, the other side of Susannah's timid, withdrawn nature.

Christine finished her tea.

'I can't wait to see Susannah performing in the drama class, first lesson tomorrow afternoon. I might have a little acting protégée on my hands. Oh, it would make such a refreshing change.' She stood up before going on, 'Especially when I know what the Head has got planned for Langley in the early New Year.'

Louisa's eyebrows rose. 'Oh, yes, what's that then?'

Christine looked mysterious, putting her finger to the side of her nose and saying, 'Ah, that would be telling.'

Louisa gathered the exercise books together and stood up, too. Break must be nearly over by now and she could no longer hear the voices of the children drifting upwards from the playground.

'Oh, come on, that's not fair,' she moaned.

Christine linked her arm through Louisa's cosily.

'All right, I'll tell you as we go.' Outside in the corridor she went on, 'It's only in the planning stage and I only know because I'm on quite friendly terms with dear Margaret outside of school. I can lay claim to some distant family connection, it seems. The Head's keen on having some foreign children over on a sort of exchange. They come to Langley and then some of our senior girls go to Norway.'

'Norway!' Louisa repeated.

'Apparently. Margaret spent a holiday in Norway last year and was very impressed by the country, especially by the way they have pulled back since the war so this idea is a pet theme of hers. She's got to convince the education committee, of course, but knowing Margaret as I do, I'm sure that won't be a problem.'

'But how will all this affect Susannah, fascinating though it sounds?' Louisa asked. 'She's only just started at Langley this term.'

'But it's the activities that would be planned for when the Norwegian girls visit. A school open day, for one, various cultural events including, and this is where I come in, a production of The Merchant Of Venice.'

'Ah,' Louisa nodded sagely, 'and you're hoping Susannah might show some talent for this planned event?'

'She'd make a brilliant Portia, don't you think?'

When Louisa remembered those dark eyes spitting fire yesterday she was inclined to agree but she only said cautiously, 'A trifle young, perhaps.'

'Age doesn't come into it. All the girls are aged between eleven and sixteen and an untalented sixteen-year-old would, in my opinion, be a complete disaster, except as a mag-nifico.'

It sounded a thrilling prospect and Louisa could not doubt Christine's enthusiasm for it.

'Of course,' Christine began in a warning voice, 'not a word to a soul or Margaret will have my guts for garters.'

'My lips are sealed.' Louisa promised her.

They had reached the bottom of the wide, sweeping staircase. The hall, with its original huge fireplace and carved coat of arms of the town of Midthorpe above it, was one of the school's many attractions.

Girls were streaming back into school after the break, chatting, laughing, quietening somewhat when they saw the two teachers. Louisa and Christine went their separate ways and Louisa pushed what the art teacher had told her to the back of her mind, only recalling it as she was walking, once again alone, back through the woods to Squirrel Grove.

She wondered when Miss Cayton intended to make public her idea or, indeed, if anything would actually come of it. Time alone would tell. Louisa rather hoped it would happen. It sounded exciting and she would like the opportunity to become involved if she could.

A twig cracking in the density of the wood brought Louisa's mind back to yesterday's incident. Were there girls somewhere around again? She stood still, listening intently. Then it came again, and again, heavier this time. Then, through the closely-packed trees she saw a figure walking quickly, not towards her but away, a man, she was certain. Could it be the same man her mother had seen hanging around?

She continued on her way seeing nothing else untoward, but she decided she wouldn't mention the man to her mother.

3

By the end of the second week of term, Louisa felt as much a part of the staff of Langley Hall as any other teacher, and she was getting on well with the girls, too, especially Susannah Priestley who continued to amaze Louisa with her creative talent.

Louisa waited to get Susannah on her own before praising her for her essay, The Black Sheep. She was all too aware that undue praise to a specific individual could cause problems amongst the other girls. Susannah, because of her shyness and nervousness, had enough difficulties in that direction as it was.

Louisa seemed to be one of the last to leave the building on most days but on that particular day she made sure she left in time to catch Susannah up as she made her way along the woodland path.

'Susannah, may I walk along with you?' she asked.

'Yes, Mrs Barton.' Her voice was low.

'Don't worry,' Louisa said with a laugh, 'you're not in trouble. Quite the contrary, I wanted to congratulate you on your essay. You've got a very vivid imagination, haven't you?'

'Have I?' Susannah didn't sound too sure of that.

'Do you like writing stories? Have you written any more?'

'A few.'

It was clear Susannah felt embarrassed talking about her writing.

'Where did the idea for The Black Sheep come from?'

Louisa tried to keep her voice light, conversational, not wanting the girl to retreat into her shell too much.

Susannah shrugged her shoulders, adjusting the weight of her satchel.

'I don't know. It just came into me head.'

'Well, Susannah, you have a talent and I'd like to help you develop it. I watched you after I'd written the words The Black Sheep on the board. You didn't hesitate, off you went, and your story is so original. You have a quite remarkable command of language for a girl your age. What does your father say about it?'

Immediately she had spoken, Louisa knew she had said entirely the wrong thing. Down came the shutters.

'He doesn't know. I don't write in front of him.'

Trying to make amends, Louisa only made things worse.

'I'm sure he'd be very proud of you, Susannah.'

'No, he wouldn't. He didn't want me to go to Langley Hall. He didn't want me to pass my eleven plus. I would have been able to leave school at fifteen and work in the mill, or better still, help him on the farm. That's what he really wants. He's always complaining he doesn't get any help. Nobody who works for him will stay long because he . . . ' She broke off abruptly.

Had she been going to say, 'Because he drinks'? Louisa didn't know what to say next. She remembered what Miss Cayton had told her and she felt sure that Mr Priestley cared deeply for his daughter, otherwise why would he have bothered to attend the pre-school interview and be open and frank about his problems? But she couldn't say any of this to Susannah because that would be to reveal that she knew the child's background and she had been sworn to secrecy. But Louisa felt she had to ask.

'Do you help much on the farm, Susannah?'

'At weekends I do. Not after school, because Dad wants me to do me homework and then go to bed early.'

School, homework, bedtime and weekends helping out. When did Susannah get any time to herself? When, for goodness' sake, did she find the time to write and she obviously did. It was all the more remarkable that her writing was as good as it was.

She must be encouraged, Louisa

determined. She might just be tempted to confide in Christine Yardley. Christine, she was sure, could be trusted and she was as keen as Louisa was to develop Susannah's creative talents.

But for now she could do nothing. Once they reached the school gates Susannah said, 'I've got to fly now, Mrs Barton. Goodbye!' and she was off, running up the steep hill in the opposite direction to Louisa's own route. Louisa watched her go.

She soon disappeared round a bend in the hill. Louisa walked slowly towards home deep in thought, but something happened that evening that drove all thoughts of Susannah out of her head.

Eileen announced as soon as Louisa got home, 'I'm going out tonight, Louisa. There's a choir concert followed by a pea-and-pie supper at the church. I've said I'll go along, give a hand with the supper afterwards.'

Eileen wasn't a regular church-goer at the local parish church, but she did attend evensong occasionally and was usually a patron of the social events. She met many of her lady customers at such events.

'That's fine, Mum,' Louisa said.

'Care to come with me?'

Louisa smiled. 'No thanks. I've got loads of homework to mark.'

She had been reading, assessing and marking for perhaps half-an-hour after Eileen left, when someone knocked on the back door. The knocking was heavy and persistent. Putting aside her book, Louisa went through into the kitchen, switching on the light as she did so. She had drawn the curtains earlier and it was pitch black outside, but she did not feel nervous, though visitors were rare after dark.

She opened the door and at first saw no-one, then a figure appeared, a tall person dressed in dark clothes. He wore no hat and had untidy hair and a beard and it was impossible to distinguish his features as the light was behind her and he seemed to be sort of hovering there, just out of vision.

It flashed through Louisa's mind that this was the man her mother had seen, also the one she had been hurrying away from in the wood, and her heart started to thump but she kept her voice steady and her hand firmly on the door, ready to shut it in his face if necessary.

'What do you want?' she asked.

'Louisa!' Just the one word in a soft, hoarse voice that she could scarcely hear.

She felt the blood draining out of her head and feared she might pass out. She gripped the door frame even harder.

'Who are you?' she demanded.

He stepped closer, into the light from the kitchen.

'It's me, Louisa.'

'Michael?'

It couldn't be! She started to sway and instantly he had moved and caught her by the shoulders. Gently he walked her back into the room and closed the door behind him. Now she saw him fully. He was dirty, his clothes were stained and creased. He didn't smell too good, but through the dirt and all that hair she recognised him.

'Michael!' she cried again, staggering to sit on one of the kitchen chairs.

'I saw your mother go out,' he said, 'so I plucked up the courage and came to the house. I'm sorry if I scared you.'

She closed her eyes and listened to him speaking. His voice was just the same, that beloved voice she had thought she would never hear again. She remembered the last time she had seen him, when he came home on a weekend pass in 1944. She remembered how she loved to watch him as he talked, how sometimes she had been unable to believe that he loved her and that she was his wife.

She looked up at him. He looked awful but so vulnerable and his dark eyes were searching her face, looking for what? Understanding? Approval? Forgiveness?

Then she burst into tears, burying

her face in her hands, sobbing uncontrollably, quite unable to stop. She heard the kitchen tap running and he brought her a glass of water.

'Here, drink this,' he said, pushing the cold glass into her hand and sitting opposite her at the table.

He didn't move or speak again. He didn't try to touch her and presently she calmed down, but she was shaking and spilling the water as she tried to drink from the glass.

'They told me you were dead,' she said in a zombie-like voice.

'I didn't know that,' he said.

Then anger flared and she glared at him.

'What happened to you? Why did you disappear like that? It's been three years, Michael. Three awful years! And look at you! Did you become a tramp? Did you suddenly decide not to come home because you didn't want to be married to me any more?'

'No, no, nothing like that.'

'Then what? Tell me, I'd really like to know.'

She was gathering courage now, the anger in her making her brave. Part of her wanted to put her arms around him, as though he was a naughty, dirty child, and tell him everything was all right, but she couldn't do that. He had deserted her; he had been dead to her. For three years he had lived not caring how she was coping without him or what she was doing with her life.

'I'll tell you everything I can,' he said, 'but could you get me something to eat first? I'm starving.'

A faint, weary smile crossed his face and for the first time since he had appeared, Louisa felt that old, familiar tug of love for him.

'You've been living rough, I take it?' she asked.

'For a while, yes. It's a long story, Louisa and you need to hear it, but . . .'

She interrupted him. 'You're hungry, and more to the point, you're filthy.' A mothering, scolding tone had entered her voice. 'I think you'd better have a bath first.'

She was glad that she had kept the fire well stoked up so there would be plenty of hot water. She got up and started to leave the kitchen, and obediently he followed her, through the hall and up the stairs. She was very much aware how close he was behind her. She showed him the bathroom, then remembered he had been in this house before and would probably know where things were.

'I'll get you something to wear,' she said, leaving him, going to her bedroom where she knew some of his clothes still hung in the wardrobe; she had never been able to bring herself to get rid of them.

When she went back to the bathroom, he had already started running the bath, and the room was hot and steamy. Without hesitation, he started to pull off his old jacket and then the flannel shirt he wore underneath. Louisa felt embarrassed and turned away, but when she reached the door, he called out her name and she had to

41

turn to look at him.

'Thank you,' he said simply, 'but I'd like you to know that later if you feel you don't want me here, I'll go.'

He was thin, pale, he needed feeding, he needed care and love and who else should be there for him but her?

'Don't be silly, Michael,' she said.

She left him then, closing the door firmly behind her. She wasn't surprised to find that her legs were trembling and she had to sit down for a few moments before going into the kitchen to get Michael something to eat. She felt slightly sick and scared. Yes, scared because she couldn't think how she could cope with this situation.

Would the authorities need to be told that Michael was back? Would he be classed as a deserting soldier, gone absent without leave? She didn't think so. She remembered that Michael had, in fact, been officially demobbed from the army. He had handed in his uniform, got his discharge papers, probably on the same day he went missing, or certainly the day afterwards, when he would have been coming home to her.

The official communications had all made this situation plain. She rubbed her hands across her eyes, feeling a headache coming on.

I must keep calm, she told herself. I must listen to what Michael has to say, but nothing had prepared her for such a situation. Through the war years when Michael was overseas, like countless other wives and sweethearts, she had often asked herself how she would cope if he didn't come home. And when he didn't, nothing had been cut and dried.

For a time she had told herself there had been some sort of military blunder, and that Michael would turn up, like a misplaced document. Later, after the final official notification, she had tried to grieve for Michael, but it hadn't been easy and hope had never faded entirely.

Now, he was back. He was alive and for the first time since she saw him standing outside the door, she began to feel excited. Michael was actually here, in the house, upstairs, taking a bath!

'He's alive!'

She spoke the words out loud and just then, nothing else seemed to matter.

4

They were fortunate enough to have a nearby neighbour who kept chickens, so fresh eggs were readily available. Together with potatoes from their own garden, Louisa was able to produce a credible plate of egg and chips, Eileen's home-made bread and a smattering of their precious butter ration completing the meal.

It was almost ready when Michael reappeared in the kitchen. Louisa was brewing a pot of tea when she heard the door open and she looked round, almost dropping the tea pot when she saw him standing there. Not only was he clean as a whistle and dressed in his own dark blue shirt and black trousers, which still fitted him well, but he was clean shaven.

'I rummaged in the bathroom cabi-net,' he confessed, 'and found a razor and some shaving cream. And don't worry, I haven't left a mess.'

The items had been saved, possibly for sentimental reasons, Louisa thought, not sure whether it could be Michael's own shaving tackle or her dad's. How glad she was now that neither she nor Eileen had been able to throw things out.

Michael's hair, though still too long, was washed and slicked back. Louisa faced him awkwardly, feeling suddenly shy.

'Smells good,' he remarked, crossing to the cooker and staring longingly at the frying chips and the sizzling eggs.

Once he started eating, Louisa wanted simply to sit and stare at him, but instead she began to wash the utensils and crockery she had been using. She could hear him making appreciative noises and by the time the washing-up was finished, Michael was through eating, sitting sipping his tea.

'Oh, my goodness, how I needed that!' he said with a contented sigh.

It would be so easy to pretend this was a cosy, domestic scene, that Michael had just come home from a day's work; so easy to go into the sitting-room and sit toasting their toes by the fire, she in the warm circle of his arms, resting her head against him. But it couldn't be like that.

Only a few short hours ago she had imagined her husband dead, but the reality was he had been living away from her, living a separate life and he must tell her why he had done that. Not until he had explained, and more importantly, until she had understood, was their any hope of a future life together.

As soon as Michael had drained his cup she said, 'Let's go and sit down and you can tell me all I need to know.'

She kept her voice deliberately cool and distant and she did not miss the sombre look that came to Michael's face.

They took chairs on either side of the fire. On the table, the homework still lay unmarked. If Michael noticed the exercise books he didn't remark on them. For a few moments, he leaned back his head and closed his eyes and because it seemed to Louise that he could easily fall asleep she called him sharply to full awareness.

'So, what is your story?' she asked.

He opened his eyes and looked straight into hers.

'Well, I'll start at the end,' Michael began. 'That might sound an odd place to start but I think I'll find it easier. You see, until just a few weeks ago, I didn't know I was married to you. I didn't even know you existed.'

'What do you mean?' she asked.

'I was someone called David and I was living in the Cotswolds. I was replacing some loose tiles on the roof of my house and I fell from the ladder and was knocked out. When I came round, I wasn't David any more. I was Michael John Barton who had married Louisa Sanderson in nineteen-thirty-nine. My home was here in Midthorpe, West

Yorkshire. I'd been demobbed from the army in nineteen-forty-five. Incredibly I hadn't forgotten my life as David but now I also remembered my former life as your husband. I left where I was and hitchhiked north. I didn't have much money on me and I didn't dare come straight to the house, so I lived rough and I hung around waiting for a chance, and also the courage, to come and face you.'

'My mother saw you,' Louisa said, surprised that she sounded so calm when her brain was careering like a carousel, 'and I think I saw you in the woods when I was coming home from school.'

Michael nodded.

'Yes, I followed you. School you say?'

'I'm a teacher,' Louisa explained briefly, not wanting to start talking about herself, only wanting to hear more of Michael's incredible story.

He made no further remark about her disclosure and went on, 'So that's the end of my story.'

'And the beginning?'

'The beginning?' Michael repeated, staring distantly into the fire. 'There was no true beginning. I can only tell that to you in the light of my remembering my past, remembering you. I remembered being at Northampton, getting my discharge papers, money, ration card. I know I wrote to you.'

'Yes, you told me about your demob clothes.'

Michael smiled suddenly and his face lit up so that once again love flickered in Louisa's heart.

'That awful brown suit!'

'Go on with your story,' she prompted him.

'After being issued with all the right things, there's a big blank in my life. The next thing I remember was being this man, David. I had a cottage in the grounds of a large, country house and worked as the gardener-cum-handyman. I knew I'd been ill, I knew I hadn't served in the armed forces because of my ill health, but I didn't know a great deal more about myself. Everything was hazy but my employer constantly re-assured me about myself whenever I had doubts and I trusted this person. So I got on with my life and my health seemed to improve. Charlie was good to me.'

'Charlie?' Louisa broke in sharply.

Once again, Michael gazed into the fire. He even picked up the poker and stabbed at the reddened pieces of coal, as though he was playing for time.

'Yes, the person I worked for, the one who owned the large house in the Cotswolds. Without their help I don't know what I should have done. I accepted my life for what it was until I fell from that ladder and discovered I wasn't David Hargreaves at all. Well, once I knew I had another life which I now remembered in vivid detail, I left straight away, and here I am. Do you believe me, Louisa?'

His last words came out suddenly, taking her by surprise. What he had told her was fantastic, but it must be true. Why would Michael lie? What could he possibly hope to achieve by turning up here after being missing for three years and tell her some fabricated account as to where he had been and what he had been doing? There had been a sort of stark simplicity about what he had told her.

'So you think you lost your memory back in nineteen-forty-five?' she asked.

'I must have done. What other explanation is there?'

'But what made you lose your memory and where did the other identity come from, and how did you manage to get from Northampton to Gloucestershire?'

She knew she was firing questions at him, but couldn't stop herself.

'Those are things I can't answer I'm afraid,' Michael said simply.

'But surely this Charlie must know something. Didn't you ever ask him?'

'No, I didn't, and not in so many words. I was there, I was David, I'd been ill and Charlie was looking after me. That was enough for me.'

He rubbed his hand across his eyes.

'Louisa, I'm so tired, I've slept in the open for the past few nights and the warmth from that fire is putting me to sleep.'

Louisa jumped up immediately.

'I'll make up the spare bed in the box-room,' she said, knowing that she was blushing. 'There isn't a lot of room in there, but Mum has the third bedroom as a sewing room. I'll get you a hot water bottle as well.'

She wondered if Michael would expect to share her room, but she knew she wasn't ready for that herself, not yet. But Michael nodded in agreement with her suggestion. He got up, too, and for a moment they were there, facing one another. Quickly Louisa moved away from him.

'And when your mother comes home?' Michael asked.

'Well, I can't pretend you aren't here, can I?'

'No, of course you can't. I don't want to make problems for you, Louisa, with anybody in authority, or anybody else for that matter.'

'What problems could there be? You haven't done anything bad or illegal. If it comes to it, you'll just have to tell anybody who wants to know what you've just told me.'

'I don't think I can stand to keep going over and over the same ground.'

'Then you don't have to,' she assured him. 'Anyway, we'll talk about that tomorrow, when you've had a good night's sleep. What happened to you is nobody's business but ours. That's what you have to keep telling yourself. And this Charlie's, I suppose. Does he know where you are?'

'Yes.'

He turned his head away as he said the word and for a moment Louisa felt certain he was not speaking the truth. Then he grinned at her, abruptly changing the subject.

'So you're a school ma'am, are you?

Tell me all about it whilst you tuck me in.'

He sounded so much like the old Michael. Louisa was beginning to feel uncomfortable, knowing that he would be sleeping just along the corridor from her and she was glad to fill the air with idle chatter about how she came to be teaching at Langley Hall, whilst Michael seemed content to sit on the chair by the spare room's narrow bed listening to her.

Louisa had a restless night and awoke feeling tired and muggy-headed. Her alarm hadn't yet gone off so she disarmed it and lay staring at the ceiling. She thought about last night, after Michael had gone to bed, and presumably to sleep, and Eileen had returned home. There had been only one way to break the news and Louisa hardly gave Eileen time to take off her coat before she announced, 'Michael's home.'

Eileen stared at her. Then she gave a nervous little laugh.

'What did you say?'

'The man you saw hanging around, that was Michael,' and whilst Eileen sank disbelieving on to the sofa, Louisa told her what had happened, and also everything that Michael had told her.

'Where is he now?'

'Asleep in the spare room. He had a bath and shaved and I made him something to eat. He was exhausted because of his living rough.'

'How can you sound so matter of fact?' Eileen demanded.

'I didn't know I was,' Louisa said, wishing her mother could see inside her head and know how it was throbbing with tension and uncertainty.

'Just as though it's the most ordinary thing in the world for your missing husband to turn up on the doorstep.'

Eileen looked nervous as though Michael's presence in the house posed some sort of threat.

'What do you want me to do? Have hysterics, tear out my hair?'

'No, no. I'm sorry if I snapped. It's

such a shock, and, of course, it must have been to you as well. I suppose it's no different from someone missing presumed dead during the war suddenly being found alive and well. In fact, it's wonderful! Absolutely wonderful!' Tears welled up in her eyes.

'Yes, it is, but I'm scared, Mum, really scared about the future, even more so than I was when I thought Michael was dead.'

'Darling, there's nothing to be scared about,' Eileen cried. 'Michael's home, safe and well. Isn't that all that counts? I know it'll be a difficult time for both of you but surely no more difficult than it would have been if Michael had come home in nineteen-forty-five.'

There was sense in what her mother had said, but adjusting to having her husband home again wasn't really what worried Louisa. Their relationship would develop and blossom slowly and naturally. In a way it would be like getting married all over again, but they loved one another and as love, affection and friendship had been the solid basis for their marriage in the first place, so it would be now.

Except that Michael had spent three years as someone else and that could not be dismissed or forgotten.

She said now, 'I'm worried about the people Michael left behind, his employer for one, this Charlie. Won't he be just as concerned about Michael's sudden disappearance as we were? Michael seemed to be close to him. I think he owes this Charlie a great deal. Michael did say that he had told his employer he was leaving, but I don't know if he really did.'

'Why shouldn't he have told him?'

'I don't know. I just got a feeling he wasn't being entirely honest with me over that. I believed his story, it's too fantastic to be anything but true, I'm sure, but there is still plenty of mystery surrounding what happened to Michael.'

'But that will be cleared up in time.' Eileen sounded very confident. 'You can't expect everything to be explained overnight, Louisa. One day at a time, remember. Isn't that how we learned to cope during the war?'

Louisa smiled. 'Yes, you're right,' she said brightly.

And they both went off to bed in a fairly cheerful and optimistic mood, but once in bed, lying in the dark with sleep seeming miles away, imagining Michael sleeping in his narrow bed, whilst her own bed seemed large and lonely, Louise felt her fear, her tension returning.

And now, at the start of a new day, the problems were still there in front of her.

She looked in on Michael before she left for school. He was still sleeping soundly, the bedcovers bunched around him. Louisa went and stood by the bed, looking down on him, listening to his deep, even breathing. She wanted to touch him, to kiss him but was afraid if she did he might awaken. It was better if he slept on till he woke naturally.

Then she would be out of the way and could leave Michael and her mother to meet and get used to one another. Perhaps it was cowardly of her but she preferred it that way. Eileen would look after Michael like a mother hen. They had always got on well together.

When Louisa got to school, there was a note on her desk from the headmistress, requesting that she stay behind after school for a brief staff meeting. She had already made up her mind that for the time being at least, she would not mention her husband's return to anyone and Eileen had promised to do the same, though Louisa acknowledged that if customers came to be measured or to collect their finished items, Eileen could hardly hide Michael under the table.

Later that morning, Christine Yardley waylaid Louisa as they were going to their respective classrooms during a lesson changeover.

'Coming to the meeting, Louisa?' Christine asked.

'Of course. Any idea what the

meeting is about?'

'My guess is it's the Norwegian business,' Christine said conspiratorially. 'The head has asked me to start thinking about The Merchant Of Venice, you know, having a read-through, to find the best possible girls for the parts. Pity Langley Hall is an all girl's school. I think you can get away with Shylock played by a female but I draw the line at Antonio and Bassanio.'

Louisa laughed again. It was good talking to Christine. She always had a bright and cheerful outlook on life.

Christine went on, 'I was right about young Susannah, you know. I let the class read part of Barrie's *Dear Brutus*. Do you know the play?'

'Yes, I do. It's one of my favourites.'

'Mine, too. Well, I chose the scene where Dearth and his daughter, Margaret, are in the wood together in the life that might have been. Remember? Now as with Shakespeare, Dearth should never be read by a female, but Susannah was brilliant as the young

Margaret, even on a first read-through. She's got to be encouraged. I could hardly credit that she was only eleven years old.'

Louisa was pleased about Susannah but a surreptitious glance at her watch told her they really couldn't stand chatting any longer.

'All right, all right!' Christine had obviously noticed her checking the time. 'Duty calls. By the way, you're looking a little peaky this morning. Are you all right?'

'Yes, I'm fine,' Louisa assured her.

Did she really look under the weather? There was nothing she could do about it even if she did. She and Christine went to their classes and Louisa knew she must force herself to concentrate on the lesson facing her. Her job mustn't suffer, because her job was nurturing and educating the girls of Langley Hall and if she lost concentration, if she allowed her thoughts to wander on to Michael, she knew she would be letting them down.

5

The meeting was held in the headmistress's study, a large room with a window which took up one entire wall, overlooking trees and beyond them the golf course.

'I'm sure there have been all sorts of speculation about this meeting,' Miss Cayton began, 'so I'll get straight to the heart of the matter. You all know I spent some time last summer in Norway. It was a wonderful experience for me but it was as much a working holiday as a pleasure trip. Whilst I was there I visited a girls school run on very similar lines to Langley Hall and the idea came to me that it would be a great experience, a great opportunity for those Norwegian girls to visit us here and, later, for our girls to go to Norway. I discussed this idea with the headteacher of the school I visited and she was as enthusiastic as I was.'

She paused to smile round at them all.

'We both agreed to tackle our respective education committees and see what could be done. And that's what I've been working on for the past few weeks. At the outset it was somewhat of an uphill struggle but I wasn't going to back down, especially when I heard from Mrs Norstrund that she had got full support and backing for the scheme. And now I've finally got the go-ahead, in writing I might add. Now, it's going to mean a great deal of hard work and preparation. The idea is that no more than fifteen or sixteen Norwegian girls will travel to Britain in the early spring and live with the families of some of our older girls. I haven't, as yet, put the suggestion to any parents but I feel sure there won't be any problem in that direction.

'Later, perhaps in the following year, our girls will go to Norway. Whilst the girls are here, I hope we can have an open day at the school which will enable all parents to be involved. We can arrange trips. The girls will, naturally, spend some of their time in school alongside their host children. It wouldn't do to let our girls run away with the idea that there'll be no school during the two weeks the Norwegian girls will be here. The idea's in the very early stages, but I've been assured of every assistance and practically carte blanche to do what I like.'

Louisa looked around her. She could see that Miss Cayton's news had met with general approval and enthusiasm and sporadic conversation broke out for a few moments until the headmistress held up her hand.

'I can see you all seem to be in favour of the plan,' she began, 'which pleases me very much. I want everyone to be involved, not least Miss Yardley who is going to be in charge of the production of The Merchant Of Venice. She has already started reading the play through with some of the girls. It is hoped we can set up a special drama club, after school hours. There'll be costumes to make and a thousand and one other things to do but I know we can work as a team. I know we can do it!'

She finished on a lofty note then invited discussion and questions which came thick and fast. Louisa looked at Christine who gave her a broad wink and a thumbs-up sign, and as the meeting broke up, came over to her.

'So there we have it,' she declared.

'Yes, you were right,' Louisa said with a smile. 'Of course, it's going to be tremendously hard work, especially if the school is to continue to be run efficiently, but I'm all for the idea,' Louisa said.

'I shall have to get some letters out to parents about the after-school drama club. I don't think there'll be any trouble, do you?'

'Perhaps some parents mightn't like the idea of their daughters going home late, especially when the nights start drawing in.'

She couldn't help thinking about Susannah. The child had given her some glimpse into her home background, and coupled with what Miss Cayton had told her on that first day, getting Mr Priestley's permission for Susannah to join the drama club might be difficult. Christine would probably airily dismiss any suggestion that Susannah might not be allowed to play Portia. That was something Louisa knew Christine had set her heart on.

Later, Louisa found her footsteps slowing down the nearer she got to the house. As she walked up the path, she saw her mother crossing to draw the curtains. Where was Michael? How had the two of them got on? Louisa had mixed feelings about seeing Michael again. He was her husband, and in the normal course of events, she would have been able to go to him, kiss him, tease him. Now she didn't know quite what to do or what to say.

She let herself into the house. There was an aroma of cooking food in the kitchen. Eileen came through from the sitting-room.

'I'm sorry I'm a bit late, Mum,' Louisa began. 'Miss Cayton called a last-minute meeting.'

'That's all right. I figured it was something like that. Supper's almost ready. I've made a liver casserole with baked potatoes.'

She went into the sitting-room and Eileen followed her. The room was empty. There was a warm fire going, but no sign of Michael.

'Where's Michael?' Louisa asked.

'He's out. He's been out for most of the day. He wanted to go and have his hair cut.'

'But having his hair cut wouldn't take him all day, would it?'

Louisa felt edgy knowing Michael was away from the house.

'Don't worry, Louisa,' her mother begged. 'Michael's a grown man.'

'Is he? What about his memory loss? What if that happens again?'

Eileen laughed nervously.

'Oh, I don't think that's likely, darling!'

'How do we know what's likely and what isn't?'

'He said himself he'd been ill, and what can he have found to do all day?'

Eileen went back into the kitchen and snatched up the oven gloves.

'Perhaps he went to Lassiter's to see his old boss.'

'I don't think so,' Louisa said. 'He wouldn't do that straight away.'

Louisa could see her mother felt guilty for having let Michael go off alone, but she was right, she couldn't baby-sit a thirty-two-year-old man. Louisa softened, went to her mother and kissed her cheek.

'I'm sorry, Mum,' she said. 'I suppose I'm just a bit on edge. He'll be all right. After all, he turned up after three years, so I don't think there's any need for us to send out the bloodhounds just yet.'

'And what was your meeting about?' she asked, changing the subject.

Louisa was just about to start telling

her when the back door opened and Michael walked in. He had certainly had his hair cut. It was in his usual short, neat style, and Louisa's heart lurched at the sight of him. Then she noticed that he looked hot, perspiring as though he might have been running.

'Are you all right, Michael?' she asked him.

He wiped his hand across his forehead and grinned at her. He looked happy and at ease and it was plain to see nothing was troubling him.

'I'm fine,' he said then turned to Eileen. 'Something smells good.'

Louisa felt bound to ask, 'Where have you been all day?'

'I'll tell you later. I'd better have a wash and change my shirt first.'

Eileen and Louisa stared at one another as he left the room.

'Just like old times,' Eileen remarked, sounding pleased.

Maybe, Louisa thought, but it wasn't as simple as that. It couldn't be. There was this big chasm in their lives that only time, tolerance and mutual under-standing could bridge. But she kept such thoughts to herself and helped her mother dish up the supper.

As soon as the plates were on the table, Michael reappeared. His flushed face had calmed and he now wore a clean, checked shirt which he must have taken from the wardrobe in Louisa's bedroom.

'Gosh, I'm starving,' he said, sitting at the table.

'Are we allowed to ask now where you've been?' Louisa asked primly.

'I've been working, on a farm.'

'Working?' Louisa repeated.

'Yes. I went into town, had my hair cut, wandered around then came back and went for a walk. I got chatting to a man in a farmyard and the upshot was that he offered me work, labouring work, so I jumped at the chance. I'm going back tomorrow. It's cash in hand, so I'll be able to help out with expenses. I haven't got a ration book, I'm afraid, but when I feel up to contacting the powers that be, that will surely only be a formality.'

Louisa couldn't understand why she felt so angry.

'You've obviously got it all worked out,' she snapped.

'What's that supposed to mean?' he asked, puzzled.

'Well, I would have thought if you wanted to work, you'd prefer to go back to Lassiter's. You were told your job would be waiting for you after the war was over, if you wanted it. I know things haven't been normal, but surely you could have waited a while till you, as you put it, felt up to it, and approached Mr Bradley. You spent three years doing an apprenticeship at Lassiter's. You're a qualified draughtsman. Why on earth do you want to work as a farm labourer?'

She saw Michael's eyes narrow. He put down his knife and fork. Eileen, too, had stopped eating and was looking slightly uncomfortable.

'You seem to be forgetting, Louisa,'

Michael began quietly, 'that I've spent the last three years of my life working as a handyman, doing all sorts of odd jobs, labouring jobs. I'm not ashamed to get my hands dirty. I was pleased when Jack Priestley offered me a job.'

'Jack Priestley?' Louisa burst in.

'Do you know him?'

'His daughter is in my class at school.'

This made things even worse. From what Louisa knew of Jack Priestley, he was often the worse for wear. Probably tomorrow when Michael turned up at Ivy Farm, he wouldn't even remember offering him work. Immediately this thought was out, Louisa was ashamed of it. Susannah's father was a good man and he was trying hard. Perhaps, she thought, on an optimistic note, Michael helping at Ivy Farm might take the pressure off Susannah.

'I need to earn some money, Louisa,' Michael went on. 'I need to be able to pay my way. I can't live off my wife and my mother-in-law.'

73

So that was it! The old, old story of her working. Louisa remembered the countless times they had argued about it. But never like this, she realised, only in the nicest possible way because when they were first married, Louisa was content to look after their little house, to look after Michael, to think about having children. So she had complied with Michael's wishes.

Now, perhaps unreasonably, it hurt her to think that Michael would consider that if he stayed home, allowed himself time to settle down, to get used to being with her again, he would be living off her earnings.

The air was fraught with tension. Michael started eating again and when Louisa opened her mouth to make some response to what Michael had said, Eileen came in with a sharp remark of her own.

'I've spent some considerable time preparing and cooking this meal,' she told them, 'and I would appreciate it if the pair of you would stop bickering

74

and offer me the courtesy of eating and enjoying the food in front of you.'

And this is what they went on to do, but there wasn't much table talk for the rest of the meal.

Soon after the washing-up was done, Eileen said, 'I'm going upstairs to do some sewing. Mrs Banks wants her dress for next week.'

It was unusual for her mother to do any work in the evening and Louisa knew very well why she was doing some tonight, but she didn't argue. Michael had already gone into the sitting-room while they were washing up and when Louisa joined him, he was reading the local evening newspaper. He had also put the wireless on and the quiet strains of some classical music provided a background to the awkward atmosphere in the room.

'You don't mind if I do my marking, do you?' Louisa asked, picking up her school bag from behind the sofa and bringing it round to the table.

'Of course not,' Michael said. 'Will

the music bother you?'

'No, I usually listen to the wireless when I'm working.'

'What made you choose English as your subject?' he asked

'I've always loved books and words, you know that,' Louisa said.

'I remember you liked to do cross-words.' He held the paper out towards her. 'Care to do tonight's before I have a bash at it?'

He was being friendly and Louisa smiled at him.

'No, thanks, you go ahead if you want to.'

He got up and rummaged around for a pencil in the top drawer of the bureau in the corner. Louisa watched him, noting the lines of his body as he bent forward over the bureau. He was tall and had always had good shoulders on him, and been fit and in the thick cotton shirt he did not seem thin as he had the previous night when she saw him in the bathroom without his shirt. She could well imagine him working on a farm. It was on the tip of her tongue to apologise to him for her earlier outburst, but she held the words back.

The clock on the mantelpiece slowly ticked the time away and Louisa was just about to remark that it was almost time to make the nightly milky drinks that she and her mother enjoyed when Michael resolutely folded up the paper and stood up.

'Done it!' he cried triumphantly.

'All of it?' Louise asked.

'Every single clue.'

'The quick or the cryptic?' she teased.

'The cryptic, of course!'

Louise got up, too, stretching.

'Tired?' Michael asked gently.

'A little,' she admitted. 'I'm going to call Mum down and make some cocoa. Would you like some?'

'No, thanks, I think I'll turn in. Jack wants me there by seven.'

It was pleasant to feel they were talking in a friendly manner.

'Michael,' Louisa began, 'I'm sorry

about earlier. I don't mind your working at Ivy Farm, if it's what you want do do.'

'It's only a stop gap, Louisa,' he said, 'until I find my feet. I just want you to give me time, that's all.'

'Of course.'

Michael moved nearer to her, then put his arms on her shoulders. She felt her body stiffen slightly and then relax and Michael pulled her closer and bent his head, kissing her on the mouth. She gave herself up to the kiss, not wanting it to end. It had been so long . . .

But when he released her, Michael said, 'Don't worry, I won't be bothering you, Louisa. I know that you, too, need time and I respect that. Good-night and God bless,' he added and was gone.

Louisa sat down, her legs weak. She touched her lips where Michael's lips had so recently been, and suddenly her eyes were filling with tears.

6

There was a restless peace between Louisa and Michael. She went off every day to school and he walked up the hill early in the morning to Ivy Farm, returning tired, hot and sometimes very dirty in the evening, but Louisa could tell that he was happy.

She knew her mother sometimes found it a struggle making their rations go three ways, but Eileen never complained. The only comment she had made was to say to Louisa.

'Is Michael fully aware that he should have a ration book?'

'Yes, he is. I'd like to ask him where his original ration book went, but I've got a strong feeling he wouldn't know and I don't want to upset him.'

Eileen agreed with that sentiment. Fortunately the rationing of bread had come to an end in July of that year and, as Eileen often baked her own bread, that was never a problem, which was just as well as Michael had asked if he could take sandwiches to work for his lunch.

So far, the neighbourhood in general had not particularly noticed Michael's presence. The houses around were mostly detached and well spread out. There were a few bungalows but these were occupied by elderly people most of whom hardly ever left their residences.

Louisa had no plans for telling any of her work colleagues. Her motive for doing so was not entirely clear to her. As far as school was concerned, so many things seemed to be happening that Louisa, whilst she was there, didn't have a great deal of time to dwell on thoughts of her husband.

First of all there was Susannah. Her essay writing continued to impress. Almost without exception, whatever theme Louisa set the class, Susannah would create a fascinating, well-written piece of fiction. Her imagination seemed to have no limits. So much so, that Louisa started to think Susannah should take her writing one step further.

She asked the girl to stay behind one day after the mid-morning bell had sounded. Susannah stood nervously by Louisa's desk.

'Does your dad get the local paper?' Louisa asked.

'Yes, Mrs Barton. We get it delivered every night.'

Louisa smiled.

'So do I, Susannah. Do you read it yourself?'

'Sometimes.'

'Then you might have noticed the Thursday evening's children's corner. Sometimes there are some very good letters in it, stories, too.'

'Oh, yes, I always read the children's corner. Do you think I should send one of my stories, Mrs Barton?'

'I certainly do. Every story printed gets a half-crown postal order.'

Susannah looked troubled.

'Could I bring it to you, Mrs Barton?' she asked. 'Would you post it off for me? I don't want to ask me dad for money for a stamp.'

'I'd be pleased to do that,' Louisa said.

Susannah went on her way apparently satisfied. The next morning she expected Susannah to turn up with a story for her to post to the newspaper but she never mentioned it and looked rather downcast. When the mid-morning bell sounded, Susannah was the first out of the classroom as though she expected Louisa to waylay her again. When Louisa went along to the staff room for her own morning tea, she found out why.

Christine came straight over to her.

'I want to ask you a favour,' she began. 'I want you to go to Susannah's home with me some time. Her father won't agree to her joining the drama group. I sent out letters as I said I would and every parent except him was thrilled to bits to give their permission. The note Susannah brought me just says he wants Susannah home straight after school. She has homework to do and he can find plenty to occupy her when she's done that. The poor child is so disappointed. Well, so am I.'

'But how can I help?'

'We can tell him how desperately we need Susannah,' Christine said. 'We can tell him this is a great opportunity for her, that nobody else can play Portia like she can and that the honour of the school is at stake.'

As usual Christine was going over the top, and Louisa had a feeling that Jack Priestley wouldn't be too conversant with Shakespeare's plays and probably wouldn't know or care who Portia was.

Louisa didn't see she had any choice, however.

'All right,' she said at last. 'When were you thinking of going?'

'Tonight?'

To have some sort of advance knowledge about how they might find

Jack Priestley, Louisa asked Michael, whilst they were eating their evening meal.

'How are you getting on with Mr Priestley?'

'Fine,' Michael said. 'He's a bit on the quiet side, a bit gruff when he feels like it, but he works hard. What do you want to know for?'

Michael seemed surprised by her interrogation, so Louisa decided to tell him where she and Christine were going that evening and why.

All he said was, 'You're not trying to tell me that that little mouse of a girl is going to be in a Shakespeare play? I've seen her once or twice and she runs a mile if I speak to her.'

'Looks can be deceptive, Michael,' she said, feeling annoyed. 'Susannah is a very talented child, very creative.'

'Well, you teachers know best, I suppose,' Michael said airily. 'And I'm sure you've nothing to worry about when you meet her father, but one word of warning, Louisa.'

'And what's that?'

'Don't patronise him, go all school-ma'amy on him. You'll only put his back up if you do.'

She had arranged to meet Christine at half-past eight. Christine had some distance to come by bus and they had both agreed it would be best to make sure Susannah was in bed before they went to Ivy Farm. Christine had told her nothing of this visit.

Because it was dark, Louisa didn't get a good look at the exterior of the farm where her husband went to work each morning. All she saw were looming, dark outbuildings, trees edging along fields. As they approached the door to the farmhouse a dog started to bark.

'Oh, he's got a dog!' Christine cried.

'Most farmers have, Christine,' Louisa said.

She knocked loudly on the door and presently she heard the sound of a bolt being drawn, and a key being turned. As the door opened slightly, a sharp command to the dog caused it to stop barking immediately.

Mr Priestley was framed in the dim light from behind him.

'Yes?' he said in a none-too-friendly manner.

'Good evening, Mr Priestley,' Christine began in her most polite voice, before Louisa herself could speak, 'I'm Miss Yardley and this is Mrs Barton, two of Susannah's teachers from Langley Hall.'

The door didn't open any farther.

'What's she been up to then?' Mr Priestley demanded. 'Must be summat serious to bring you round at this time of night.'

'Susannah's not been up to anything, Mr Priestley,' Christine assured him. 'We've come to talk to you about her being allowed to join the drama group. May we come in?'

'I've written you a note and I've got nowt else to say about it,' came the terse response.

'Please, Mr Priestley!'

It was clear that Christine wasn't going to be put off. Louisa admired her tenacity. The door opened wider.

'Oh, come on in then, I don't expect I shall get any peace till you've had your say.'

They stepped inside the large, square room. The black and white dog was lying on the rug before the meagre fire and although it wagged its tail feebly, it didn't move. Louise saw Jack Priestley properly for the first time.

He was about fifty-five, she supposed, a big man, ruddy faced with plentiful grey hair brushed back from his forehead. He was neatly dressed and clean shaven and seemed perfectly sober, but Louisa could not fail to notice the whisky bottle and glass on the table in the centre of the room, though the bottle wasn't open and the glass was empty. Of course there was nothing wrong in a man having a drink in his own house, especially after a hard day's work.

'Susannah's in her bed long since,'

Mr Priestley announced.

Christine smiled. 'We thought she would be.'

He hadn't invited them to sit down but Christine did so anyway, advancing into the room and sitting on a couch facing the fire range. Louise decided to do likewise and it didn't seem to bother the man, though he himself remained standing, his arms folded across his chest.

'What's all this palaver about being in a play?' he asked. 'What does my Susannah know about acting? She's gone to that school of yours to be educated, not to act in plays.'

'But, Mr Priestley,' Christine said with infinite patience, 'taking part in dramas, understanding the great classics, is just as important as reading, writing and arithmetic. And Susannah is so talented. Please give your permission,' and she went on to describe at great length about why the drama group was being formed in the first place, telling Mr Priestley about the planned Norwegian visit, even waxing lyrical about war-time camaraderie and international friendship.

Louisa was amazed at Christine's oratory skills, but they certainly seemed to sway Susannah's father and Louisa could see him visibly weakening.

He rubbed his hand across his face.

'I don't know,' he wavered. 'In another couple of weeks it'll be dark early. I can't let my lass come through them woods in the dark.'

'But I said in my letter that no girl would have to do that. The school will take full responsibility for their safety and, in Susannah's case, I will take personal responsibility.'

After several moments when even Christine didn't say a word, Mr Priestley said, 'Well, I must admit things have got a bit easier around here and I don't have to ask Susannah to lend me a hand as much as I did, not since that young chap came along.'

He was referring, of course, to Michael, Louisa realised.

Mr Priestley went on, 'Oh, go on then! But, if I think Susannah's school work is suffering in any way, that'll be the end of it.'

'Oh, Mr Priestley, thank you, thank you,' Christine cried.

They didn't stay long after that and as soon as they got outside Louisa said, 'Well, I can't think why you needed me here. I haven't said a word!'

'Moral support, Louisa,' she said, linking her arm through Louisa's. 'He seemed nice, didn't you think? There've been tales circulating about him, you know. About him and drink apparently. Did you notice the bottle?'

'Of course I noticed it, Christine,' Louisa said rather crossly, 'but he seemed sober as a judge to me. A thoroughly nice man, in fact.'

Louisa offered to walk with Christine to the bus stop and when she got home eventually, she found that both Eileen and Michael had retired and the house was dark and empty. Now that she was alone after the bustle of the day, she was acutely aware of her loneliness and of the fact that despite their seeming to be getting on, she and Michael were still worlds apart.

7

Louisa saw a bright-faced Susannah when she came into the classroom the next morning. The thirty girls got to their feet, as they always did when a teacher entered.

'Good morning, girls,' Louisa greeted.

'Good morning, Mrs Barton,' they chorused before resuming their seats.

Louisa took the register call and then they started to leave the classroom to join the rest of the school for morning assembly in the gymnasium. As the girls filed past her in a neat row, Louisa pulled Susannah to one side. The girl grinned at her.

'You seem happy this morning, Susannah,' Louisa said.

'Yes, Mrs Barton, I am. Dad's letting me be in the play. Thank you.'

'And you really want to do the part of Portia?'

'Yes, I do.'

Louisa could see the girl was very excited by the prospect.

And, she thought, her father had not kept their visit to the farm from her.

'And what about your story?' she asked.

'Oh, I've already sent that off, thank you. Dad gave me the money for the stamp after all.'

Was there a new understanding between father and daughter? Louisa hoped so as she watched Susannah go off to catch up with the other girls.

On the following Friday the school broke up for half-term. Louisa was looking forward to the break but wished she and Michael would be able to spend more time together. As it was, with him working every day at Ivy Farm, she wouldn't be seeing much more of him than she already did.

She still hadn't been able to persuade him either to try to contact somebody in authority about what happened to him, so that he could at least be issued with the official documents he ought to have, not the least a ration book and an identity card, and he wouldn't go to Lassiter's engineering works either.

Louisa tried not to let Michael see how much his stubbornness upset her. However, when he came home from work on that Friday of the half-term break, he was grinning from ear to ear. He even grabbed her in his arms and swung her round the room.

'Michael!' she cried. 'Put me down!'

But secretly she was pleased. They had very little physical contact. He always kissed her good-night now and if she was up before he went to work, and she wasn't always, he kissed her goodbye in the mornings. She had accepted their friendship and knew she would never be the one to take it a step further, and sometimes it saddened her that if Michael felt the same way she did, what hope was there for them?

Now, as he released her, she said, 'And what's got into you today?'

'I'm having a holiday,' Michael

declared. 'And it was Jack's idea. He knew it was half-term, of course, because of Susannah and he told me to take a few days off, spend some time with me missus!'

Louisa went cold.

'Mr Priestley knows you're married to me?' she asked.

'Of course, why shouldn't he?'

Then did Susannah know, too?

'I haven't told anybody you're back, Michael,' Louisa said quietly.

'Why not? Are you ashamed of me?'

'No, of course not.'

There was that distance between them again. And really, Michael was right — why shouldn't people know her husband was alive and well? He had done nothing wrong. It wasn't as though he was an army deserter. People would be pleased for her, but in the back of Louisa's mind was the knowledge that she and Michael weren't living as man and wife and she was afraid this might come out. She couldn't face the sorrowful looks, the whispers that she was sure would follow such a revelation.

'Tell people, please, Louisa,' Michael said.

She was afraid he wouldn't want to spend the half-term break with her now, but before long he had cheered up again and was even suggesting they might go away for a couple of days.

'Go where?' she asked, a feeling of excitement coming over her.

'Anywhere. The seaside.'

Louisa couldn't remember when she last went away on holiday. Eileen was a home-bird and Louisa wouldn't go away without her. She heard her mother coming down the stairs.

'We'll talk about it later,' she said. 'I want to tell Mum what we're planning to do first.'

'Of course,' was all Michael said. 'I'd better go and get cleaned up before supper.'

Had his voice cooled? They were both so touchy with one another. They never used to be like that. Theirs had been such an easy relationship. Would they have been like this anyway, after being parted by the war years, even if Michael had come home in 1945?

Louisa remembered the days after peace in Europe had been declared. The excitement she had felt, the anticipation of Michael's return. She had devoured his rare letters, laughed at the things he had said, glowed with his expressions of devotion to her.

Their love for one another hadn't changed, had it? Certainly hers for Michael had not. So why couldn't she simply forget he had had another life she knew nothing about? Why couldn't she accept he was home again, which was all she had ever wanted? Why couldn't she simply throw her arms around him and say how much she still loved him? The barrier still remained but at least now there was the prospect of spending a few days alone together and that was enough to give Louisa hope.

Monday of half-term week started off

as a glorious, golden October day. Soon after breakfast, when Eileen was preparing for her first customer, teasing them that she didn't have the time to sit about doing nothing, Michael said, 'Do you know I haven't yet seen this school of yours, Louisa? Are the woods closed to the general public?'

'No, I don't think so,' Louisa said. 'There are gates but to my knowledge they're never even shut, let alone locked.'

'Then you can go for a walk with me this morning. The exercise will do you good.'

Louisa laughed.

'I get plenty of exercise walking through those woods twice a day!'

'And I don't really need any exercise either.' Michael said smiling. 'Jack's a real slave-driver.'

He didn't mean it. He always spoke about Jack Priestley with affection. And it seemed the liking was mutual. Perhaps Jack had benefited by having someone like Michael to work for him.

Perhaps Jack had felt lonely, bereft after his wife's tragic death, unable to confide in anyone, letting the work at his farm get on top of him, using drink to dull his mind and keep him going. But Jack had not been drinking lately, of that Louisa was sure. And there had been a subtle change in Susannah, too.

'I won't be able to take you into the hall itself,' Louisa said now.

'Never mind. I can peep through the windows.'

He seemed in a very good, light-hearted mood this morning, maybe because of their planned holiday.

They set off towards the entrance to the woods, a stroll of perhaps five or ten minutes. Soon, Michael took hold of her hand.

'You don't mind?' he asked, looking at her.

'I don't mind,' Louisa assured him.

They didn't talk much but there was no need for words.

'Look!' Michael cried suddenly, pointing to his left. 'A squirrel!'

Louisa was just in time to see the bushy-tailed creature skimming effortlessly up a tree.

'I gather there are lots of them,' she said.

'Hence the name Squirrel Grove, I suppose,' Michael said. 'It's certainly a nice setting for a school.'

They were nearing the bend now, where Susannah had been about to be tossed into the holly bushes. How long ago that seemed. So much had happened. And then, the path narrowed, the trees grew less and there was Langley Hall set out before them, fronted by the playground which doubled up as a netball pitch.

'My, some place you've got here, Louisa,' Michael remarked in awe.

'Yes, I know. That's my classroom up there,' she pointed to a first floor window.

He put his arm around her shoulders.

'I'm very proud of you, you know that? Making a career for yourself.

Something I don't suppose you would have had if I hadn't gone missing.'

It was the first time they had mentioned that in some time.

'Oh, I don't know,' Louisa teased. 'I might have got tired of simply being a little housewife before long.'

'You were never simply a little housewife to me, Louisa.'

She felt shy and linked his arm, urging him forward.

'Come and look at the stables,' she said.

'Stables! Don't tell me equestrian events are on the school curriculum.'

'No, but we have a handsome science lab and gymnasium.'

They entered the cobbled yard through the opening in high, stone walls where huge gates must once have stood. The former stables were in an L-shape, single storey. The windows were fairly high up but Michael was tall and managed to look through them.

'You've got the lot,' he said, 'horizontal wall bars, a wooden horse. I'm impressed.'

They walked around the entire building and finished up in the school's pride and joy, the Italian Garden.

'Don't ask me what makes it Italian,' Louisa said.

'Who takes care of the school and gardens?' Michael asked.

'The school caretaker and a very reliable team of workers. The caretaker and his wife, a very nice couple, live in a lodge house but that's at the end of the other drive, where the main gates are. We won't walk that far.'

They started to walk back the way they had come. Now Michael walked with his arm around her waist, and presently she slipped her own arm around him.

'It's so quiet,' he remarked. 'Hard to imagine it's a school grounds.'

Louisa found she was resting her head against him and wasn't really surprised when Michael stopped walking, turned her to face him and started to kiss her. It was nothing like his brotherly good-night kiss. There in the woods, alone, private, they gave in to their pent-up emotions.

When they finally drew away from each other, Michael said hoarsely, 'I love you, Louisa. I want us to be like we used to be. I don't want there to be any barriers between us. I've been thinking, you're right, I should go to Lassiter's and ask for my job back, but I can't do that yet. Jack needs me. Do you know about his wife?'

'Yes, and about his drinking.'

'Well, he doesn't seem to do much of that as far as I can see. He talked to me, Louisa, he told me all about himself and how he'd sort of neglected his child. He's trying very hard to make it up to her, and I can't leave him just yet. But I will, I promise, when I think the time is right. Jack knows I won't be there for ever, because he knows all about me, too.'

'Everything?' Louisa asked.

'Everything. And I want you to know, darling, that after we've been away I'm going to contact whoever there is to contact, a doctor, perhaps, to try to get to the bottom of what happened to me. Can you be patient with me a little longer?'

'Oh, Michael, just take your time, I'm with you whatever you decide to do. I love you so much.'

They went back to the house and Louisa was sure her mother would notice the change in them. Louisa knew that Michael would never again have to sleep in the box room.

8

Louisa was smiling when she left Miss Cayton's study and made her way to the staff room. Refreshed from her half-term holiday, knowing that things were well between her and Michael, seeing Susannah returning to school a much less nervous, edgy child and glowing from the success of her short story in the children's column of the newspaper — and now she had told the headmistress everything.

'My dear, I'm delighted,' Miss Cayton had cried. 'What wonderful news! So nice to hear that something that appeared to be a tragedy has turned out so well. I wish you and your husband all the very best for the future.'

Yes, it was wonderful, and now, with the passing weeks, when it seemed that Michael had never been away from her, Louisa had put things into perspective

105

and Michael's missing three years did not seem to matter. He was still working at the farm, but he had been to see his old boss at Lassiter's, and was also in the process of communicating with the former War Office about his missing papers.

Life felt good to Louisa. Now, before the news spread amongst the other teachers, she wanted to tell Christine herself. The staff room was quite crowded as the teachers gathered for their morning break but Louisa wanted to be alone with Christine.

'Let's go for a walk,' she suggested, taking her coat from its hanger. 'I want to talk to you, in private.'

The playground was crowded, with Miss Russell, the games mistress, as the teacher on yard duty that morning, looking chilly and blowing on her fingers. The girls, of course, didn't seem to mind the cold, running about, laughing, chatting.

Louisa and Christine set off in the direction of the Italian Garden.

'I bet this is the only school in Midthorpe to have an Italian Garden,' Christine said proudly, 'but I'd rather be out here on a hot, summer's day. It's freezing.'

Louisa decided to plunge straight in with her news.

'My husband's come home,' she said.

Christine stopped walking and stared at her.

'What?'

'Yes, I know it's unbelievable but it's true,' and she went on to tell the same story she had previously told the headmistress.

Christine seemed to have completely forgotten how cold she was.

'Oh, Louisa.' She threw her arms around her friend and hugged her fiercely. 'Am I the first to know?'

'Except for Miss Cayton, and Susannah.'

'Susannah?'

'Michael's working at her father's farm.' And this was another story to tell. 'Michael was more open about what happened than I was. We went away for a few days during half-term, Michael and I.'

'Oh, gosh, a sort of second honeymoon, was it?'

Louisa laughed.

'Well, we didn't have a first honeymoon, really,' she confessed.

'Where did you go?'

'Only to Bridlington. Nowhere posh,' Louisa told her. 'Just a nice little boarding house, but we did lots of walking on the beach and the cliffs.'

In the evenings they would sit in the cosy, little parlour with the handful of other guests who were staying at the boarding house, chatting, playing cards. The holiday had been totally relaxing and Louisa knew that she and Michael had become as close as they had ever been.

'So miracles do happen, don't they?' Christine said, starry-eyed. 'I wonder when Mr Right is going to come along for me.'

'No-one waiting in the wings?' Louisa asked.

Christine made a snorting sound. 'Some hope!'

Because Christine was shivering with cold, they started back to the warmth of the school building, though break wasn't quite over.

There was always such a feeling of joy now when Louisa heard Michael come in after a day's work. She would run and kiss him, and he would hold her close. Eileen, too, was delighted.

One evening, after supper, Michael surprised them both by saying, 'I've been thinking that perhaps we should be looking for our own place.'

They both stared at him and Michael laughed.

'Don't look at me like that,' he cried. 'What's wrong with the idea? You're earning good money, Louisa, and although at the moment mine's only cash in hand, that will change when I go back to Lassiter's.'

'You're definitely going to do that?' Louisa asked.

'Well, Mr Bradley's already offered

me my old job back, and he's prepared to sort out the business of an insurance card, so, yes, I think I'm about ready to make the move. Jack and Susannah are getting on so much better. He talks about her all the time and he's thrilled to bits with her success with her short story writing. She's doing some poems now.'

Louisa smiled. 'Yes, I know that,' she said.

'Of course, you're her teacher! Then there's the forthcoming Shakespeare play. Susannah's working hard on that. I just feel the time is right for me to settle down in a proper job. And having our own place would be nice, too.' He looked at his mother-in-law. 'What do you say, Eileen?'

Eileen laughed nervously and Louisa could see her mother wasn't too keen on the idea of being left alone, but she also knew Eileen was not the sort of person to stand in their way or make a fuss, and now that Michael had brought the matter up, Louisa was bound to agree that, yes, it would be nice to have their own home again. Somewhere near, she wouldn't consider moving too far away from her mother.

'Of course,' Michael began, 'it won't happen overnight, you know. It'll probably be next spring or summer before we find somewhere suitable that we can afford. Houses don't grow on trees.'

Eileen relaxed.

When they went to bed later, they promised themselves they would start looking that weekend, after they'd got Friday's evening paper which had a list of any properties to rent in the area.

Louisa said, 'If we can stay in Squirrel Grove so much the better. What other area of Midthorpe has such a romantic name!'

Michael put his arm around her and kissed her.

'I'll find you a palace, darling,' he whispered.

Louisa knew that any home, however small, would be a palace if she shared it with Michael.

It was Saturday morning when the visitor arrived. Michael had gone into Midthorpe for a haircut and also to follow up one or two possible property details. Eileen was at the home of a client, doing a fitting for a mother-of-the-bride outfit, and Louisa, after washing her hair, was sitting in the front room, brushing her hair and idly contemplating what they could have for lunch.

The caller rang the front door bell which was a surprise in itself as most people came to the back door. However, Louisa put down her brush and went to answer it. When she had unlocked and opened the door she saw a tall woman standing there, a very well-dressed young woman, maybe a couple of years older than she was. She had the most beautiful golden hair, worn loose around her shoulders, and carefully-applied make up. The colour of her hair perfectly matched the autumn browns and golds of her tweedy two piece suit. Her legs were long and slender and she wore dark brown court shoes.

Louisa was not usually given to staring so hard at people, especially at someone calling at the house, but she couldn't stop herself.

The young woman smiled. 'Good morning,' she greeted.

Louisa pulled herself together.

'Good morning,' she returned. 'May I help you?'

'I'm hoping so. I'm looking for a Mr Michael Barton. He does live here, doesn't he?'

Louisa nodded, with a feeling of apprehension. Who was this person?

'Yes, he does,' she said and noticed that the woman looked relieved.

'Oh, good. Of course, I knew he did. I was just being polite. Do you think I could come in?'

'Michael isn't home at the moment. May I ask what you want with him, Miss . . . ?'

'Menton. Charlotte Menton.'

She held out her hand and reluctantly Louisa took it. The fingers were long and slender inside the beige kid gloves.

'Look,' Miss Menton went on, 'I do think it would be better if you allowed me to come in. Are you Mrs Barton by any chance?'

Louisa nodded, unable to speak. She was beginning to feel increasingly uneasy about this serene, lovely woman on her doorstep.

'Then you'll want to hear what I have to say, I'm sure.'

Louisa wasn't at all sure that she did, but it was clear Miss Charlotte Menton wasn't going to go away until she had got what she wanted, so Louisa opened the door wider and let her visitor enter. They went into the sitting-room. Eileen had lit the fire earlier and Louisa was glad that everything was neat and tidy.

'What a lovely room,' Miss Menton said.

She sat down without invitation, crossing her elegant legs, removing her gloves and laying them neatly down on top of her brown leather handbag on the arm of the chair. Louisa went to sit opposite her. Under normal circumstances, she would have offered her visitor a cup of tea, but these weren't normal circumstances. She waited for Miss Menton to speak.

'I know this is going to be very difficult for you, Mrs Barton,' she eventually said and her face took on a sympathetic look. 'And I would much have preferred Michael to be home, but as he isn't, I feel I must explain myself in his absence.'

'Please do,' Louisa said quietly.

'First of all, I've brought these.'

She removed her gloves from the bag, opened it and produced some folded papers which she handed across to Louisa. Louisa stared at her.

'Please look at them, Mrs Barton,' Miss Menton urged.

Louisa did so. She saw at once that they all related to Michael, his demob papers, his ration card, his identity card. Her heart started to thump.

'Where did you get these?' she

demanded in a shaking voice.

'From Michael, where else? You see, Michael and I lived together from nineteen forty-five till he left me suddenly a few weeks ago.'

'You're lying,' Louisa cried, but she knew it wasn't a lie, because suddenly it all made sense — Michael's disappearance, his sudden reappearance, his claims that he had lost his memory and he had been working as a gardener/handyman in some large, country property. His employer . . . oh, no, he had given the name of his employer as Charlie!

'You're Charlie, aren't you?' she asked.

Miss Menton's lovely smile returned.

'That's right. Well, at least that's what Michael always called me,' she said. 'He was the only person who ever called me that.'

9

Louisa decided to offer her visitor tea after all. She rushed into the kitchen, filling the kettle, water splashing into the sink as her hands shook. The next thing she knew Charlotte Menton was standing close behind her.

'I'm sorry if I've upset you,' she said.

'Why have you come here?' Louisa asked.

'To see Michael, of course, to find out what he wants to do.'

'What he wants to do?' Louisa repeated, pushing past Charlotte and going back into the sitting-room. 'He's come home, hasn't he? Isn't that enough for you?'

Charlotte smiled. Her smile, lovely though it was, was beginning to irritate Louisa. It seemed too sweet, too out of place for the situation they were in.

'Not really,' she said, sitting down,

this time on the sofa.

Louisa did not sit. Foolishly, she felt if she stayed on her feet it would give her some sort of advantage over her visitor.

'Michael's regained his memory and whatever life he was living with you is over. You had no right to come here,' she said.

'I didn't know he had ever lost his memory. Is that what he told you?'

A heavy, despairing weight was settling in Louisa's stomach. She wanted this woman to leave, to turn back the clock and for this terrible thing not to have happened. When Louisa didn't say anything, Charlotte went on.

'Michael's lied to you and I'm sorry about that, but you can see why he did it. He didn't want you to know about me. He didn't want to upset you.'

Well, that was certainly true. Michael had referred to this woman as Charlie, deliberately letting Louisa think his employer was a man. She probably wasn't his employer at all, another lie.

'Mrs Barton,' Charlotte went on, 'I haven't come here to cause trouble.'

'No?' Louisa shot at her. 'And what about David?'

'David?' Miss Menton looked puzzled.

'Michael told me he had lived three years as David Hargreaves, that he'd been ill and he'd come to believe as he got better that he was this David.'

'I know nothing about that.'

Whom could she believe? Louisa's head was in turmoil. Why should Michael make up such a story if it wasn't true? On the other hand, why should Charlotte Menton be lying now?

The kettle started whistling and Louisa went to brew the tea, glad of a few moments alone. This time the visitor did not follow her. Louisa presently went back into the sitting-room, carrying a tray which she set on the low table in front of the sofa.

'Milk, no sugar,' Charlotte said amiably.

Louisa forced her hands to remain

steady as she poured the tea.

'If you were so idyllically happy in this life of yours, why did Michael leave you and come back to me?' Louisa asked next.

'That's what I'm here to find out,' was the calm reply.

Before they could start to drink their tea, Louisa heard the back door opening and shutting. It could be her mother returning and she half hoped it was, but it turned out to be Michael. When he walked into the sitting-room, looking somehow boyish and vulnerable after his haircut, he stood there, his face gone suddenly pale, staring at Charlotte Menton.

She got up and crossed quickly to him.

'Michael!' she cried and would, Louisa was sure, have thrown her arms around him if he hadn't moved rapidly away from her over to the other side of the room.

He looked scared and Louisa's worst fears were realised.

'What are you doing here, Charlie?' Michael demanded. 'How did you know where to find me?'

'Easy,' Charlotte began airily. 'I had your papers, remember, and your address was on them.'

Michael's face looked grim and he seemed to have regained his composure.

'So you know I'm Michael now, do you?'

'I've always known that.'

'What are you talking about? I was David to you. Since I regained my memory, I've been able to understand something of what happened. I don't know how I lost my memory in the first place, but perhaps you do, Charlie. Whatever, I now know it was you who fed me the false identity of David Hargreaves, telling me I'd been ill, and I believed you. For three years. I believed you because I didn't know any better. But now I do.' He turned desperately to Louisa who had been standing there, listening to the two of them, watching them. 'What's she been telling you, Louisa?'

Before Louisa could speak, Charlotte came in with, 'I've been telling her the truth, about my meeting you when you were on the run from the army, about how I gave you shelter, that we fell in love and were going to be married!'

Louisa felt as though her head might explode. She was hearing more and more, both from Charlotte and Michael. He had never said before that he believed Charlotte had fed him a false identity. He had never been able to give a logical explanation of how he came to be David and she had accepted his lack of proper knowledge, or at least she had pushed it to the back of her mind, so happy to have Michael back, so happy that their life had now been able to continue.

Now she was forced to face the situation full on. They all were. Louisa suddenly found a new strength, a new determination. No more lies, no more half-truths.

When Michael yelled at Charlotte, 'I

never deserted the army, I was demobbed like everybody else. I know that as well as I knew my own name,' Louisa cut him off in midstream.

'But you don't really know that, do you?' she said. 'And I'm sick of being in the middle here, one of you saying one thing, one another. Somebody must know the truth!'

She was surprised by the look of calm that suddenly crossed Michael's face. He moved and went to sit in an armchair, but he kept his eyes firmly on Charlotte.

'Perhaps Nicholas does,' he said quietly.

Nicholas? Not somebody else for goodness' sake, Louisa thought!

She saw the hesitant look on Charlotte's face and she, too, came to sit down again. She was nervous now, picking up her gloves and fiddling with them. Whoever this Nicholas was, the very mention of his name had disturbed her. Michael seemed to have produced a trump card.

'Leave my brother out of this, Michael,' Charlotte said.

'How can I? I trusted him, too, as I trusted you, because he was a doctor, a psychiatrist. I met him that day when I was leaving, after I'd regained my memory. Didn't he tell you? He pulled up alongside in his car as I was going down the drive. I told him what had happened. I told him I knew I wasn't David Hargreaves and that I was going home to my wife.

'He asked me how you'd taken it, Charlie, and I said you'd been very angry, that you'd said I'd promised to marry you, but I never made such a promise, not as David, not as Michael, not ever. I worked for you, I owed you something, or at least I thought I did, for looking after me. But not any more.

'You're a liar, Charlie, and now I believe you always were. Nicholas said to me that afternoon, 'Try to make allowances for Charlotte, she's been very unhappy in her life and since you came, it's as though she's been reborn,' but he still urged me to leave and said I was doing the right thing. I shall get in touch with Nicholas. His Harley Street telephone number shouldn't be difficult to trace, and I shall ask him, beg him to tell me the truth.'

There was silence after Michael's long speech. His words had carried conviction and Louisa's belief and trust in her husband were returning. There was much he hadn't told her that he could have, she knew that now, but she also knew beyond the shadow of a doubt that he didn't love this woman, that he had never loved her and certainly had never promised to marry her. To let him know how she was feeling, Louisa crossed to Michael's chair and sat on the arm of it, putting her hand on his shoulder. He smiled up at her.

'It'll be all right darling,' he said fervently.

Charlotte stood up abruptly.

'Nicholas is abroad at the moment,' she stated jerkily.

'I can wait. I've learned to be patient these past few years,' Michael said.

'In any case, he'll never say anything against me. He's my brother and he loves me. He's cared for me since I was a little girl.'

'I'm sure he has.'

Charlotte gathered up her bag and gloves, clutching them in front of her as though afraid someone might snatch them away.

'Take care, Michael,' she said, 'that matters don't blow up in your face.'

With those final words she was gone. Louisa looked out of the window and saw her striding down the drive. There was no car pulled up outside so she didn't know how their visitor had arrived, but she watched Charlotte turn to the left and walk away briskly. Then she stood up and faced Michael.

'I was scared, Michael,' she said, 'she was so convincing and her words seemed to make so much sense.'

Michael stood up, too, taking hold of her hands.

126

'I'm sorry, Louisa, for putting you through all this.'

'It isn't your fault.'

'But it is. I could have been completely honest with you from the start. I deliberately misled you into thinking Charlie was a man. I never mentioned her brother to you, or that we'd had that blazing row on the day I left. As far as the rest of it is concerned, well, I've tried to be as honest as I could be and I don't suppose the mystery of what happened to me is any clearer now than it was.'

'Do you think contacting Charlotte's brother really might help?'

'Yes, I do,' Michael said, 'He's an eminent doctor, a good man, I'm sure, but there were times during those three years when I got the feeling he wanted to tell me something, when he was almost on the brink of speaking. And then he would withdraw. It's only now, with hindsight, that his behaviour seemed significant. You see, I never questioned who I was. As far as I was concerned, I recovered from an illness and carried on with my life as David Hargreaves, but obviously I wasn't this person, so both Charlie and Nicholas must have known that.'

He rubbed his hands over his eyes as though they were aching.

'I don't know, it just seems to get more complicated. We'd just started rubbing along rather nicely together, you and I, and now this. Charlie turns up out of the blue. But she knew exactly what she was about, that's for sure.'

'What do you think she'll do now?' Louisa asked. 'Will she come back?'

'I hope not. I think I scared her mentioning Nicholas like that.'

Louisa had thought that, too. She kissed his cheek.

'I love you, Michael,' she said simply.

'I don't deserve you,' he whispered, his arms around her.

'Don't say that!' she scolded.

They heard movement in the kitchen. Eileen had returned. Quickly, Michael said, 'Don't say anything to your mother about any of this. I think that's best for the time being.'

Louisa agreed, though deep down she thought keeping it all from her mother would just be another furtive secret and she would have preferred to have been open and honest about it all.

10

It was on the day that Michael started work at Lassiter's Engineering Works that a letter arrived from Dr Nicholas Menton.

Michael came into the kitchen, wearing his pre-war dark blue suit, white shirt, pale blue tie. How smart he looked, Louisa thought, looking at him proudly! How handsome!

'Will I pass muster?' Michael asked, smiling at Louisa and Eileen.

'Very dignified,' Eileen remarked.

Michael grimaced.

'Oh, dear, I don't know if I like the sound of that,' he said.

Louisa came and kissed his cheek.

'Are you nervous?' she asked.

'A little,' Michael confessed. 'It's the first time I've worn a suit for years.'

'What about your demob suit?'

'Did I ever get to wear that, I

wonder. I must have done, I suppose, when I left that camp in Nottinghamshire. Interesting point, Louisa. Whatever happened to that suit?'

They had seen no further sign of Charlotte Menton, but Michael had been as good as his word and had written a letter to Charlotte's brother, Nicholas, after finding his London business address through enquiries at the post office. Some time had elapsed since then, but Louisa remembered Charlotte saying her brother was out of the country and preferred to think that was the reason for his silence, rather than that he had declined to answer.

And now the time had come for Michael to take up his old position as draughtsman with the prestigious firm which had branches in other towns besides Midthorpe.

Louisa knew that morning that her husband was indeed nervous because he could hardly eat any breakfast, merely nibbling on a slice of toast and marmalade, where he would have normally eaten a plate of eggs and bacon with relish, especially since he had started work at Ivy Farm.

'I'll help out on odd weekends,' Michael had promised him, and Louisa was sure he would because he had really taken to both the outdoor life and to Susannah's father himself.

Michael was ready to leave the house before Louisa herself set off for Langley Hall. He would walk to the main road and catch a bus into town, from where he would take another fifteen-minute walk to the engineering works. He would finish at five-thirty.

Louisa and Michael stood in the doorway saying goodbye. Louisa felt almost as nervous as Michael did. She looked up at the sky.

'Looks like being a nice day,' she said.

'Good, I don't fancy getting drenched,' Michael said.

'You've still got your umbrella,' Louisa reminded, 'for when it does rain.' He bent and kissed her on the mouth.

'Wish me luck.'

Louisa gave him a hug.

'All the luck in the world,' she cried.

'And, don't forget, if anything comes in the post, open it, even if it's addressed to me.'

Louisa nodded. 'I will.'

He was referring to Nicholas Menton's letter, of course, though he did not say so.

She watched him walk along the path and disappear round the side of the house and she ran into the sitting-room to watch him through the window until she could see him no longer. He walked tall and erect, with a purpose in his step and Louisa felt a strong rush of love for this man with whom she had vowed to spend her life. She prayed at that moment that Dr Menton would get in touch and that he would be able to shed some light on what had happened to Michael, but in her heart she was not sure that he would. If he had been able to do so, why had he not come forward sooner?

Michael had said Nicholas Menton knew he was leaving and the reason why, but he had simply let him go and surely he must know that his own sister was about to make a journey up north to contact Michael.

Louisa was forced to leave for school without knowing if post of any kind was delivered. She had told nobody at Langley Hall, not even Christine, about the new developments in her life, but when she meet Christine that morning, she did say, 'Michael's started his new job today.'

'At Lassiter's you mean?' Christine asked. 'Well, if he settles in as well as you did here, Louisa, he'll have no problems.'

As Louisa went to her own classroom, she reflected on how the time had passed so quickly since her first day as a teacher, and on how Susannah Priestley had changed, too, in the same period of time. She was bright, friendly and open and had made lots of friends. And, according to Christine, all her potential as an actress was being fulfilled as she worked hard on the rehearsals for play. In fact, the whole school was working hard towards the visit of the Norwegian girls, an event which was coming nearer and nearer.

That morning, Louisa's thoughts were continually straying to Michael. How was he? How was he coping? What time would he be home? Would he be exhausted? Would he be pleased with how the day had gone?

The English lesson with her own form had just started and Louisa was sitting at her desk, totally unaware that she was staring into space when she heard someone saying, 'Mrs Barton, are you all right?'

Louisa pulled herself together with a jerk. Nancy Carter, the form captain, a popular, friendly girl was standing by the desk wearing a worried look.

Louisa smiled.

'Yes, thank you, Nancy. Now let's see,' she began, fiddling with the papers on her desk. 'Perhaps this morning we could . . . '

A hand shot up from the back of the class.

'Yes, Maureen?' Louisa said.

'Please, Mrs Barton, can we hear some of Susannah's new story?'

'Oh, yes, please, can we, Mrs Barton?' other voices chorused.

Louisa glanced at Susannah who was blushing but also looking pleased.

'So you've written a new story, have you, Susannah?' she asked.

'Well, I'm trying to write a long story, about a boarding school,' Susannah said.

'Do you mean you're writing a book, Susannah?' Louisa asked.

'Yes, Mrs Barton.'

Louisa was impressed. She scanned the eager faces before her. Of course, she should be following the normal curriculum, but she was as keen as anyone to hear what Susannah had written.

'Would you like to read some out to us?' she asked.

'I don't mind,' Susannah said quietly.

'Come to my desk then,' Louisa offered.

Susannah got up from her seat, taking a red-backed exercise book out of her desk. She read in a clear, confident voice. Louisa watched her, finding it hard to believe that this bright and self-assured child was the same who had started at Langley Hall at the beginning of term. She had certainly found her niche and her artistic talents seemed to know no bounds. Whether it was acting or writing prose, or even poetry, her natural talent shone through. Louisa was so pleased that Susannah was proving to be one of the most popular girls in the class, too.

She wondered idly where Susannah's gift had come from. Had her natural parents been artistic? With all due respect to Mr Priestley, he could not possibly be the one responsible, there being no blood tie between him and his adopted daughter. Miss Cayton, quite properly, possibly because she herself did not know, had given Louisa no information about Susannah, other than the fact that she was not the Priestleys' natural offspring.

When Susannah finished reading, the girls applauded her and Louisa joined in.

'My word,' she said with a smile, 'you certainly know how to hold people's interest, Susannah.'

'Thank you,' Susannah said shyly, and returned to her desk.

The rest of the lesson proceeded as normal.

It was already starting to come dark when Louisa set off through the woods after school was over. The kitchen welcomed her with the aroma of baking and the warmth from the cooker. In the sitting-room, a huge fire was roaring and Eileen had already drawn the curtains against the gathering darkness. When Michael came home, they would eat their evening meal.

'There's a letter, Louisa,' her mother announced.

Louisa glanced at the mantelpiece where any post was usually propped. She saw the official-looking cream envelope with the typed address.

'Is it . . . ' she began, not daring to go and pick it up.

'Yes, it's from Dr Menton. And Michael said you needn't wait for him to open it,' Eileen gently reminded her.

Louisa went and picked the envelope up, turning it over in her hands. Then she got a letter-opener from the bureau and slit the envelope open, unfolding the thick cream paper inside. She read the contents through silently at first then out loud to her mother.

Dear Michael, she began, *I was surprised to receive your letter regarding my sister, Charlotte. Perhaps not surprised that you felt the need to contact me, but because of Charlotte's visit, which, I can assure you I knew nothing about, as I was in Geneva at the time. In view of the contents of your letter, I feel it imperative that we meet. I can travel to Yorkshire in a few days. If my suggested arrangements are suitable, please do not feel the need to contact me further. I look forward to seeing you again, Michael, and to meeting Mrs Barton. I remain, yours faithfully, Nicholas R. Menton.*

'Oh, dear,' Louisa began, refolding the letter and replacing it in its envelope, 'I'm not sure I'm looking forward to Dr Menton's visit.'

'But perhaps he can throw some light on the mystery,' Eileen said.

'Perhaps it's a case of letting sleeping dogs lie,' Louisa said wryly. 'Michael and I are getting on so well. I don't want things to be spoiled.'

Eileen gave her a hug.

'I'm sure they won't be. And remember, darling, Michael must really want the air to be cleared, especially after what you told me about Charlotte Menton's visit.'

Her mother was right, of course, and Louisa was certain her husband would agree, but still she couldn't help dreading the doctor's visit in just under two weeks. He had chosen Saturday morning, possibly because he realised they both worked during the week. Of course, Dr Menton worked too, though he must be rather more a free agent than they were.

What would he have to tell them? Would any revelations he had to make really set her and Michael's minds at rest?

11

Dr Nicholas Menton arrived at the house promptly, emerging from a sleek grey car on the dot of half past ten. Louisa watched him from the bedroom window before going downstairs to join her husband. Eileen had left the house earlier.

'You don't want me around,' she said. 'I've got customers to visit.'

Michael was already opening the front door when Louisa got downstairs, even before Dr Menton had rung the doorbell. He gave her a brief smile.

'Here goes,' he said.

Nicholas Mention was a striking figure, tall, well-dressed, with the same golden brown hair as his sister. His eyes, too, were like hers, tawny gold. As soon as he came in the door, Michael grasped his hand and shook it warmly.

'Good to see you again, Nicholas,' he greeted.

They went into the sitting-room.

'This is Louisa, my wife,' Michael introduced her. 'Louisa, Dr Nicholas Menton.'

His smile was warm, putting Louisa immediately at her ease as he shook her hand. His grasp was firm and strong.

'How do you do?' he said.

'Pleased to meet you,' Louisa returned. 'May I take your coat?'

'Thank you.'

Dr Menton unfastened the buttons of his dark overcoat, removed it and handed it to her. Louisa went and hung it at the bottom of the stairs. When she went back into the sitting-room, she urged the doctor to take a seat, as both he and Michael were still standing, possibly awaiting her return.

Michael said, 'It's good of you to come, Nicholas, I really appreciate it. I hope it wasn't too inconvenient for you.'

'Not at all. I've managed to combine

this visit to see you, Michael, with an appointment I have in Leeds tomorrow afternoon.'

He looked at them both with a smile.

'I can see you've settled down well, Michael,' he said.

'Yes, I'm fine. I've started at my old firm again.'

'Good. What is it you do?'

'I'm a draughtsman in an engineering firm.'

'A far cry from a gardener-cum-handyman then.'

'Would you like some tea, Doctor Menton?' Louisa asked tentatively.

'No, thank you, not just at the moment, and please, call me Nicholas, Mrs Barton.'

'Then you must call me Louisa,' she said.

'That will be my pleasure. I can't say how sorry I am that Charlotte came to see you like she did. She was left alone in Snowshill, of course, apart from the housekeeper, but I had no idea she was planning to do what she did. She seemed to have settled down well after you left, Michael. Of course, she was very upset at first, but I calmed her down, and I thought I had made her understand why you had to leave, but apparently I was wrong. How much do you know of what happened, Louisa?' he asked her.

'All, I think,' she told him. 'I believe Michael has told me all he knows.'

'I have,' Michael said earnestly.

'I believe you, Michael,' Nicholas said, 'but you see, you don't know the whole story, do you? You remember only what Charlotte told you, what she wanted you to believe. Isn't that the truth of it?'

'I suppose so.'

'And now it's up to me to fill in the gaps, as it were. I can only say how deeply sorry I am that I wasn't honest with you right from the outset. I am deeply ashamed of the way I behaved, but you see in the beginning my only thought was to protect Charlotte and by the time I realised what was happening, it seemed to be too late. The die was cast. You believed yourself to be David Hargreaves and I couldn't see a way to extricate myself from the deception I'd allowed myself to become a part of.' He paused and looked at them. 'Am I making myself clear?' he asked.

'I think so,' Michael answered, turning to Louisa. 'Louisa?' he queried.

She nodded, saying nothing, but what Dr Menton was saying wasn't very clear to her. She felt nervous, apprehensive, as though something awful was going to be revealed. Perhaps it was.

Nicholas went on, 'You see, my sister, Charlotte, was always a very highly-strung girl, even as a child. I practically brought her up, being fifteen years older than she is. I spoiled her. My family is quite rich, though I don't say that with any intent to boast or patronise. Charlotte has had every advantage money could buy. Whatever she wanted I would obtain for her. She went to the best schools. I bought her the house in Snowshill, the horses, the cars. I am sure our war years were spent in a very different way from yours. Because of my profession I was never engaged in active duty. That's not to say, of course, that I didn't do my bit in helping the war effort.'

He explained no further what he meant by those last words and Louisa didn't mind because whatever Nicholas Menton did or did not do during the war had no bearing on what happened to Michael.

'At the time Charlotte met you, Michael,' Nicholas went on, 'I was in London, where, as you know, I have my private practice. I generally try to visit Gloucestershire at the weekends, but at that time I had had to spend a couple of weeks in the capital, so, Charlotte was left virtually on her own. When I returned, I found she had dismissed our housekeeper, who, incidentally I have recently re-installed, and you were there, Michael. Before I start to tell you Charlotte's own explanation of what happened, I'd first like to tell you about Charlotte's experiences. As I've already said, she was always very highly-strung, prone to fits of alternating high exuberance and low depression. She wasn't exactly manic and often an extravagant gift from myself could raise her sense of well-being in a trice. Coping with her exuberances was sometimes less easy. However, I was a doctor and if I couldn't help my own sister, of what use was I?'

It was a rhetorical question. The doctor continued.

'Now I'll explain the background to what happened. It won't excuse what Charlotte, and myself, of course, did, but it might explain it in some way. When she was twenty-one, Charlotte met a young man, a local landscape gardener and to put it simply, she fell head over heels in love with him. She brought him to the house, ostensibly to do some work in our grounds. His work was excellent and I liked him very much both as a craftsman and as a man. At first I had no idea he and Charlotte were becoming involved, and when she suddenly sprung it on me that they were getting engaged, I was amazed. He was just finding his feet in his chosen profession, and though I had no reason to doubt he would go far, I couldn't see how he would be able to provide for Charlotte as I had always provided for her, as our parents before me had always provided for her every need. I tried to explain my feelings to my sister, but she reacted strongly and said she was going to marry David whatever I might think.'

'David?' Michael broke in sharply.

Nicholas smiled.

'Yes, David, David Hargreaves. I knew my sister well and I knew she would follow up on her threat to run away with David and that I would never see or hear from her again if I tried to stand in their way. I couldn't allow that to happen. Apart from the deep love I have for my sister, I felt her nature was too vulnerable, too unstable for her to cope away from her familiar, family environment, so I gave in, as I always had with Charlotte and she and David became engaged. For a time they were blissfully happy and I began to think I had been wrong to try to oppose them. David was a wonderful person and he seemed to have a truly good influence on Charlotte. Her erratic moods steadied down. She was a regular visitor to David's home in Snowshill.' He turned to Louisa. 'For your benefit, Louisa,' he said, 'that's the name of the small village near where we live. Our house is very isolated and it was this very isolation that played a large part in what happened when Michael came along. As I was saying, David lived in the village, with his elderly, widowed mother to whom he was devoted. They were starting to plan their wedding, with my blessing of course, when something terrible happened. David contracted leukaemia and became desperately ill.'

Louisa reached for Michael's hand,

as Nicholas went on.

'Charlotte moved in with Mrs Hargreaves to help care for David. She hardly slept day or night for weeks. I was very worried for her, but I never tried to interfere because I knew it's what Charlotte wanted to do. But no-one could help David, I'm afraid, and he died. It took a very long time for Charlotte to recover after that, indeed there were times when I thought she would never recover, but she did and we picked up the threads of our lives.'

Louisa's heart went out to poor Charlotte, for the first time feeling sympathetic towards her. The story continued.

'Now I'm practically up to date, Michael. Charlotte became deeply involved with her horses and as you know, she ran a riding school for young people, a very successful venture for her. She also bought and sold horses and had some of her stallions out for stud. She travelled a great deal and this seemed to agree with her. I felt I could give her more independence and was not nearly so worried about her volatile nature as I had been before she met David. It seemed as though that young man had instilled some of his own calmness and self-control on my sister. Soon after the end of the war, Charlotte went to Northamptonshire to look at some young mares.'

Northamptonshire, where Michael went to be demobbed! The connection was being made at last.

'She was towing a horsebox at the time, though, as it happens, she didn't buy any horses at all. On a winding, country road she was in a collision with a young man who was walking towards her. According to what my sister told me, she rounded a bend and there he was, and the accident was unavoidable. Charlotte stopped, of course, and went to the man's assistance. He didn't seem too badly hurt, but had sustained a bad blow to the head and was semi-conscious. In the normal course of events, Charlotte should have gone in search of assistance but when Charlotte bent to aid the young man only one thought was in her mind. He was the spitting image of her late fiancé, David, and all her feelings for David came back to her, overwhelming her. Of course, you know that that man was you, don't you, Michael?'

'It must have been.' Michael looked and sounded stunned. 'Though I can't remember going for a walk. I do know the camp was in a country area though.'

Nicholas continued his story. 'Somehow, Charlotte managed to get you into the back of the horsebox, lying you down on the clean straw in there. Then, instead of taking you to the nearest hospital, she drove all the way back to Gloucestershire and home. There she looked after you, making you comfortable, nursing you. It's something to be thankful for, I suppose, that you didn't have any broken bones or any other serious injury, or I dread to think what the consequences might have been. As it was, once you started to improve, it was obvious to Charlotte that you couldn't remember anything about the accident, or indeed, anything about who you were. I like to think that Charlotte did not so much scheme and plot, as merely take advantage of what occurred. By the time I returned home, you were up and about and to all intents and purposes you were David. Charlotte believed you were David and so did you. You knew you'd been very ill, and you were still somewhat groggy, and why should you question what you'd been told?'

Once again Nicholas paused in his narrative, looking at Louisa and Michael, serious and unsmiling.

'This is the part of the story where I became involved. I cannot excuse myself, but I want you both to remember what I've already told you about my sister, her vulnerability, her volatile nature, her devastation when David died. When I got home, she told me quite calmly that David had come back, and when I first saw you,

Michael, I must admit I was shocked at the resemblance to David, but, of course, I knew you weren't him. Charlotte told me about the accident. I kept gently questioning you whenever I had the opportunity, and came to the conclusion that you had suffered amnesia, but Charlotte had done her work well in the time you and she were alone in the house. As far as you were concerned, you were David Hargreaves. Why should you question it? I should, of course, have put a stop to it all there and then but I didn't. I couldn't.

'I didn't know then that Charlotte had found papers on you making it obvious you were recently demobbed from the army. Indeed, I only found out about that after you'd left, Michael. To all intents and purposes you were an unknown, amnesiac young man. I saw nothing in the newspapers about you, and all I knew was that once again Charlotte had found her David. You might find it very difficult to believe that a professional person like myself, a well-respected man of medicine, could go along with a sick girl's fantasies, but that is what I did. You took over the lodge at the bottom of our drive and started to work as gardener-cum-handyman.'

'And this went on for three years?' Louisa said in astonishment.

'Unfortunately, yes, it did.'

'But, Michael,' Louisa turned to him, 'when Charlotte came here that day and announced you and she were to be married, you denied any of it.'

'Because marriage between us had never been mentioned, I swear it, Louisa,' Michael cried, 'and remember, Charlie called me Michael all the time she was here. She knew the truth. She knew it all along.'

'Of course she did, Michael,' Nicholas agreed, 'but my sister wasn't concerned with the truth, only with having David back in her life, and that's why I helped her to keep you there. I've already told you Charlotte had got rid of the housekeeper, and because of our isolation we were able to keep to ourselves, but I promise you, Louisa, that there was no question of romance between Charlotte and Michael. I agreed to go along with Charlotte on that proviso. I knew you weren't David, I knew you must have a family of your own somewhere. Oh, I didn't know whether or not you had a wife, but there was always that possibility, and I wouldn't allow Charlotte to let you believe she was your fiancée. We had endless rows about it, but I stuck to my guns and Charlotte was so scared she might lose you again that she agreed to my terms.'

He smiled faintly.

'It seems in the long run she was content just to have you there, being able to see you every day of her life. To her it was simply a miracle.'

'Until the day I fell off the ladder,' Michael said, 'and suddenly remembered who I was and everything about myself.'

Nicholas nodded.

'Oh, what an unholy mess,' he groaned. 'And where is Charlie now?'

'At home. I have engaged a nurse to care for her. Well, now you know everything and I hope you can both forgive me for what I did.'

Michael held out his hand.

'I can see why you did it,' he said softly.

They shook hands, then Dr Menton shook hands with Louisa.

'I'm very sorry,' he told her.

Louisa put her arm around Michael's waist.

'I've got my husband back,' she said, 'and that's all that matters to me.'

She felt sorry for Charlotte. She was ill, there was no doubt about that. Hadn't her brother as much as admitted it? But it was all over now. She and Michael could get on with their lives and look forward to a future together.

When the doctor had left, they were both silent for a few moments, sitting next to one another on the sofa. When

Michael slipped an arm around her shoulders, Louisa rested her head against him.

'Thank you for being so understanding,' he murmured. 'We must try not to let it spoil our lives. Think of it all as part of the wartime experience.'

Louisa thought that was a good idea. People had coped with and survived much worse things. They would, too, together.

12

And so, life went on. Michael had settled down at Lassiter's; Louisa was nearing the end of her first term at Langley Hall. They were still looking for a suitable place to live, but as Christmas came nearer and the right house hadn't come along, they decided to wait until the new year.

Louisa couldn't remember being so happy and often reflected on how fortunate she was. Who would have thought only a few months ago that not only would she and Michael be re-united, but that they would be closer and more in love than ever?

There were times, of course, when sad thoughts about her father came over her. She would glance across at her mother, and she would think, if only Dad could have come back, too, and she would realise how brave her mother was not only to have made a life for herself alone without her beloved husband, but also to be so happy, so thrilled for Louisa and Michael. My mum and Michael, Louisa thought, the two people I love most in the world. She would never take either of them for granted.

And so Louisa was totally unprepared for the afternoon she got back from school and found Eileen crying. She was in the sitting-room, huddled in a chair, holding something in her hands, sobbing quietly.

'Mum!' Louisa cried. 'What on earth's the matter?'

She saw that her mother was holding the photograph of Colin, her dead brother, Louisa's uncle. Eileen looked up with tear-filled eyes.

'Oh, Louisa!'

'Tell me, Mum, please,' Louisa coaxed.

Eileen made an effort to control herself, dabbing at her eyes with her handkerchief and Louisa waited patiently. At last Eileen spoke.

'I've got something to tell you,' she began haltingly, 'something I should have told you years ago. Something I never wanted you to know, but now I have no choice.'

'Then tell me, Mum. Surely whatever it is can't be so terrible.'

Eileen went on, looking at the photograph in her hands, the smiling young man who had died so tragically young.

'There's only one way to say this, Louisa. All these years you've been believing a lie. Colin didn't die from some illness. He took his own life.'

'What?' Louisa got up abruptly.

'Please sit down, Louisa. I'll feel better if you're sitting down.' Eileen sounded calmer now and Louisa did as she was told.

'Colin hanged himself,' Eileen stated bluntly.

It didn't make sense. Louisa had been nearly sixteen years old when her uncle died. She recalled the sadness in the family, her father comforting her mother; the black clothes they wore; the day of the funeral.

'Why are you telling me this now, Mum?' she asked quietly.

'Because I had a visitor today and she's coming back tonight and I knew before she did, you and Michael had to know the truth about Colin. I'm sorry it's happened this way, Louisa. I know it was wrong of me to let you believe a lie, but you were so young, just a child, and I couldn't bring myself to tell you that your uncle had committed suicide. Your father wanted me to, he felt it was wrong to keep the truth from you, but I insisted, not only because of the terrible thing Colin had done, but because of why he did it, and after that, later . . . well, there didn't seem to be any point in changing my story.'

'Until now,' Louisa said wryly. 'Because of this woman. Who is she? Why is she coming here?'

Eileen took a deep breath.

'Her name is Cecily Hallam. She

gave birth to Colin's baby when she was seventeen years old.'

Louisa had not expected this. It was a shock, but why had he felt the need to kill himself because a girl had had his baby?

'Cecily came from a very well-to-do family,' Eileen explained. 'It's a mystery to me how she and Colin ever got to know one another, but they did. Of course, no-one in either of the families knew anything about the relationship until it was too late and the damage had been done. Cecily's father wouldn't hear of her and Colin getting married. As soon as he found out, he packed his daughter off to live with relatives, we never knew where, and he vowed the baby would be adopted. Colin was devastated. He really loved that girl, Louisa. He would have made a good husband and father.'

'Go on, Mum,' Louisa prompted gently.

'Colin wrote to Mr Hallam several times, he told me that, begged to be allowed to see Cecily. He wrote to Cecily, too, and he couldn't understand why she never answered his letters.'

'But if Cecily had been sent away . . . ' Louisa put in.

'I know, and I tried to make Colin understand that, but it didn't do any good. He couldn't take the agony of not only losing Cecily but losing his child, too. So he put an end to it all.'

Such a heart-rending story, but still Louisa couldn't understand why Cecily Hallam had suddenly come into their lives nearly twelve years later. And how, indeed, had she found out where Eileen lived?

'Apparently, Cecily's father had died recently. She lives in America,' Eileen explained. 'She told me she's an actress over there. She's very beautiful, I can't deny that. Well, she's come over here to settle her father's estate. She's an only child, you see. She spoke about some letters. They must be the ones Colin wrote, but I wasn't really taking it all in, Louisa, not when she told me who she was. She was very upset, too, because it was only through the letters she'd found out that Colin was dead. What a terrible shock that must have been for her!'

'And the letters, why have they suddenly come to light?'

'It was Mr Hallam's housekeeper,' Eileen said. 'She found the first letters, torn up in a waste paper basket and she managed to make out what they said. When the later letters arrived, some addressed to Cecily herself, of course, she recognised the handwriting and kept them from Mr Hallam. She never opened those later letters, but she told Cecily she'd decided to keep them for her until such time as it was prudent to let her have them. Now, of course, the old man is dead and poor Cecily wants to know what happened to her baby, especially now that she knows Colin is no longer alive.'

Eileen covered her face with her hands.

'Oh, dear, what a tragedy. I think

about my brother often, you know, but now this has brought it all back and I've had to tell you. But I don't know what happened to the baby, Louisa,' Eileen cried. 'I only know it was adopted, and that it was a little girl. Cecily told me that. They took the baby from her as soon as she was born. Isn't that a terrible thing to do?'

'It certainly is,' Louisa agreed. 'You say Cecily is coming here again?'

Eileen nodded.

'Yes, tonight, but I can't help her in any way, can I? I told her you weren't aware of the true facts about your uncle's death and that you must be told before she came here again, and I said, I half promised that I'd tried to help her to find out what happened to her baby, but what can I do?'

Louisa didn't know what to say to comfort her mother. It seemed an impossible situation. Eventually, Eileen said, 'Well, if I don't get a move on, there'll be no supper tonight and Michael will be home soon.'

'Don't worry about that,' Louisa said. 'I'll give you a hand. I know it's been a terrible ordeal, Mum, but I'm glad I know the truth now.'

But, later, when Louisa told the whole story to an astounded Michael, she asked him, 'How can we help that poor girl, Michael? Where do we start?'

'I don't know, I'm afraid,' Michael said. 'I suppose there are adoption societies, things like that, but if we don't know the baby's name, or the names of the people who adopted her, our hands are tied. Could the house-keeper know something, do you think?'

'I shouldn't think so. If she did, surely she would have told Cecily.'

They sat in silence for a few moments. Eileen had gone upstairs. She had been quiet throughout their evening meal and Louisa knew her mother was nervous about Cecily Hallam's next visit to the house. Perhaps she wouldn't come, after all. Perhaps she would realise they wouldn't be able to help her.

But in the next instant Louisa realised this was unlikely. Eileen Sanderson was the only link to the father of Cecily's baby. Quite simply she did not have anyone else to turn to.

Michael said, 'I'm puzzled as to how Miss Hallam knew where to come.'

'So was I,' Louisa told him, 'but Mum said Uncle Colin's last letter to Cecily, that terrible letter where he told her he was going to kill himself, also gave Mum's name and this address. Somewhere for Cecily to go, Uncle Colin said, if she needed help. And, of course, she's done that now but was never able to do it sooner because she didn't have the letters. Her father must have been a terrible man, to treat her like he did, to send her away, to attempt to destroy Uncle Colin's letters.'

Michael put his arm around her shoulders. 'He must have thought he was doing what was best for his daughter. She was so young, he must have believed he had to protect her. And the child will probably have been brought up in a stable home, with parents who love her.'

Louisa knew all that, but it did not make her any the less sorry for Cecily Hallam or any the more charitable towards her father, though he was dead now and obviously beyond anyone's reproach.

'The girl will be going on for twelve now,' she mused.

'Yes,' Michael said softly.

They fell silent and were startled when the front door bell rang loudly. As Louisa got up to answer it, her mouth suddenly gone dry, she found Eileen coming down the stairs.

'It's all right, Louisa,' Eileen said, 'I'll let Miss Hallam in.'

She seemed very calm and Louisa went back into the sitting-room to join Michael. Louisa heard voices before her mother appeared.

'This is Miss Cecily Hallam,' she said. 'Miss Hallam, this is my daughter, Louisa, and her husband, Michael.'

The woman stepped into the room.

She was tall, slender, wearing a pale trenchcoat and high-heeled shoes. She had short, bobbed glossy dark hair with a bright red beret perched on the side of her head. She was very beautiful, just as Eileen had said, but as Louisa stared at her face, at those lovely dark eyes, she knew instantly where this woman's child was.

Cecily Hallam was the spitting image of Susannah Priestley!

What could she say? What could she do? She glanced at Michael, but he was shaking hands with Cecily, smiling at her and it was obvious he hadn't seen what she had seen. But then why should he?

Louisa tried to relax. She and Michael sat on the sofa, Eileen and Cecily took the armchairs.

'I'm so sorry to bother you all in this way,' Cecily began.

She had a slight American accent, Louisa realised, an attractive, soft voice. An actress, Eileen had said. Well, wasn't Susannah an actress, too? She could also write, and so could Uncle Colin. Louisa remembered his beautiful poems. So Susannah got her gifts from her parents. What could be more natural? Eileen was speaking. Louisa forced her eyes away from Cecily's face to listen to her mother's words.

'You're no bother, dear. I only wish we could have met under happier circumstances. Your father dying . . . ' Her voice trailed off.

'But my father's death wasn't half as much a shock to me as finding out about Colin.' She glanced at Louisa. 'Of course, I know that must have been terrible for you, too, Louisa. Your mother told me you'd never known the truth about your uncle.'

'No, I hadn't, and of course I never knew you and Uncle Colin had a child. I'm so sorry, Cecily.'

Cecily gave a tremulous smile.

'Did your mother tell you I never even held my baby? I went to America soon after. My father had distant relatives there. I went to theatrical school, which was something I'd always wanted to do. My father would never have allowed me to go on the stage, but my American great aunt was much more liberal and she positively encouraged me when she knew what I wanted. I don't want to boast, but I'm quite successful, too.'

'Will you go back to America?' Louisa asked tentatively.

'I expect so, eventually. Fortunately I'd just finished a play when I heard about my father's death, so I don't have to rush back if I don't want to.'

What would she say, Louisa asked herself silently, if I told her that her daughter was at this very minute living in a house not half an hour's walk away? But she couldn't say that, not just yet. She had to talk to Susannah first, and to Mr Priestley, of course. Could she disrupt their lives in that way, and she did not fool herself into thinking their lives wouldn't be disrupted. Hadn't Jack Priestley suffered enough, losing his wife in a tragic accident? How could she be the one who might cause him to lose his child, too?

But then there was Cecily to consider. Through no fault of her own she had had to give up her baby at birth. True, she had made a life for herself and, by all accounts, had a very successful career in America, but no woman who had had a child would ever be able to forget her.

Her mind was racing. It was heart-breaking to hear her mother say, 'We've talked about it a great deal, Cecily, and it seems we're powerless to help you. My husband and I were never informed of what happened to you or your baby. Of course, now that we've met you, I hope we'll be able to keep in touch, by letter, at least. You could so easily have been Colin's wife.'

She broke off when she saw that Cecily was becoming upset again.

'I know you can't help,' Cecily sobbed, 'and I'm so grateful you've let me come and talk to you all. It was just a wild hope I had, that after all these years I might be able to find my baby.'

Louisa had to really force herself not to speak out.

'You will leave us your address, won't you?' she asked. 'We'd like to see you again whilst you're here.'

And for the moment she had to be content with that. Now she had to pluck up courage to talk to Jack Priestley. But first, Louisa made up her mind that she would at least tell Michael what she had guessed, when they were in bed that night. She could do no more at present.

Next evening, at a time when they could be reasonably certain that Susannah would be in bed, Louisa and Michael set off up the hill towards Ivy Farm. It wasn't unusual for Michael to visit his former employer, now his friend, though Louisa had never gone with him before, but they hadn't told Eileen why. Until Jack Priestley had been informed of what was going on, Louisa felt it was unfair to say anything to anyone else except Michael.

'Perhaps it might be as well if I did the talking, Louisa,' Michael suggested. 'Jack knows me. Oh, I know you've met him, but I'm sure you'll agree that he isn't the easiest person in the world to get on with.'

'I think he's changed though, Michael, from what he used to be,' she said, smiling up at him. 'I think he became more mellow after you went to work for him. Susannah certainly is a much happier child than she was. And now we're going to tell him his daughter's natural mother has turned up. How will that make him feel? I don't know if I can go through with it.'

'You must. You owe that to Cecily at least.'

Michael was right, but that didn't stop Louisa from feeling very uneasy and nervous as they approached the farm. Michael knocked on the door, and when Jack opened it and saw who it was his face broke into a smile.

'Eh, lad, this is a nice surprise,' he

said, opening the door wider.

When Jack saw that Louisa was there as well, his smile wavered somewhat.

'Mrs Barton,' he greeted shortly, nodding his head towards her.

But he ushered them inside and asked if they would like to take their coats off.

'I can offer you tea, lad, but nowt stronger, I'm afraid. I seem to be short on spirits and the like these days.'

This was good news!

'We don't want anything, Jack, thank you,' Michael said.

They were sitting on the old settee in front of the wooden dresser. As Jack sat down in what was obviously his favourite armchair he said, 'You've come for a reason, I take it. My lass not in bother at school, I hope?'

'No, no, of course not.' Louisa hastened to assure him.

Michael coughed.

'There's only one way to say this, Jack,' he began, 'and that's to come right out with it. We know that your daughter, Susannah, is adopted . . . '

Jack broke in rather sharply with, 'Well, so what? I've never made no secret of that fact and the lass is well aware herself that she's adopted.'

'But what you don't know, Jack, and neither did we until a couple of days ago, is that Susannah's natural father is Mrs Barton's, Louisa's, uncle.'

Jack got up abruptly and turned away from them. Louisa could see his fists were clenched tightly.

'What nonsense is this, lad?' He was trying to make light of what he had been told. 'We, my Hannah and me, never knew who Susannah's parents were, so how can you know?'

Michael commenced to tell Mr Priestley all about Cecily and Colin and of the events of the last few days. As he spoke, Jack remained silent, though he did come back and sit in his chair again.

When Michael finished speaking, Jack burst out, 'And what proof have you got that my Susannah is this Miss

Hallam's daughter? She's got no official papers, I take it. Well, I have. I've got Susannah's adoption certificate and it's signed by a judge, I'd have you know.'

He was getting agitated and once again Louisa wondered at the wisdom of coming here to this man's house, upsetting him as they so obviously had.

'Mr Priestley,' she said, 'there's no doubt, and once you see Cecily you'll know it's true. She and Susannah are so much alike.'

Jack turned angry eyes on her.

'And what makes you think I'm gonna see her? I can assure you I'm not. She can't lay any claim to my lass, not after all these years, she can't.'

Once again Michael spoke in a calming voice.

'Cecily Hallam doesn't want to take Susannah away from you, Jack. She only wants to be allowed to see her. Put yourself in her place. She was forced to give up her baby against her will. It's only by the purest chance that she found out what happened to Colin as

179

well. She was so devastated when she knew Colin was dead, to deny her access to Susannah now would be so cruel, so unfair . . . '

'Cruel? Unfair?' Jack yelled so loudly Louisa dreaded that he might wake Susannah up which must be avoided at all costs. 'Do you know how many times my Hannah cried herself to sleep because she couldn't have a baby of her own? Do you know what she felt like when she first took that baby into her arms, or what we went through when we'd to wait three months before we went before that judge and Susannah was officially ours, and then another six weeks after that in case the natural mother changed her mind? That's unfairness, lad, that's cruelty in my eyes.'

'But, Jack,' Michael persisted, 'none of that was Cecily's fault. Can't you see that? We could, of course, never have come here and told you about Cecily and Louisa's Uncle Colin. We haven't told Cecily yet that we know where her child is because at the end of the day,

Jack, that will be up to you. Yours will be the last word. If you say no, then so be it. Cecily will be none the wiser. She'll go back to America and I don't suppose we shall ever see her again.'

'And I suppose she'd be wanting to take Susannah to America with her,' Jack said bitterly.

'In the future, yes, she very well might, for a visit. But she wouldn't take Susannah away from you. You're her dad and will always be her dad. Cecily knows the position. She knows she has no parental rights.'

Jack fell silent. Louisa held her breath waiting for him to speak.

Eventually he said, 'I lost my missus, as you know. It would break my heart to lose my lass as well.'

'You won't lose her, Jack, that I can promise you,' Michael said.

Jack heaved a great sigh, one of resignation, as though he was beaten.

'It would depend on what Susannah said. If she's agin the idea, then that's that.'

'Of course.'

'And if she's gonna come here, this young woman, I can make any arrangements myself. Give me her address, and a telephone number, if she has one. You don't have to be involved.'

'But we are involved,' Louisa started to say, but Michael's hand on her arm, firmly, stopped her.

'Fine, Jack,' Michael said, standing up. 'We'll leave it up to you, then.'

'Aye, and I'm making no promises, mind you.'

Michael held out his hand. 'Fair enough.'

They shook hands. Jack didn't offer Louisa his hand. They got their coats and left almost without saying another word. Louisa said nothing, linking her arm through her husband's.

It was well over a week before they heard anything further. Louisa was on tenterhooks every time she saw Susannah, waiting for the child to show some sign that her father had told her about Cecily, but Susannah seemed just the same, working hard, chattering on about Christmas, getting excited about the forthcoming school party, as everyone was.

Had Jack perhaps changed his mind about contacting Cecily? Was he simply going to sit back and do nothing?

Then came the letter, addressed to Eileen, neat, unfamiliar handwriting. For once, the post came early and although Michael had already left for work, Louisa was still at the house.

'I wonder who it's from?' Eileen pondered.

Eileen sat at the kitchen table, reaching for a clean knife and slicing open the envelope. She unfolded the expensive-looking notepaper, glancing at the signature at the end of the letter.

'It's from Cecily,' she said.

Louisa sat down then.

'What does she say?' she asked.

Eileen scanned quickly through the letter, a smile coming to her lips.

'It's all right, Louisa,' she said, 'I think everything will be all right.'

Dear Mrs Sanderson, she read out, *I thought I must write to thank you, Louisa and Michael for what you have done to help me and to tell you that I have seen Susannah! Mr Priestley, Jack, contacted me and we arranged a meeting after which, on Sunday, I went to Ivy Farm and saw Susannah. Perhaps I should say first that when Jack first met me he said, 'Why, my lass is the spitting image of you, young woman!' And when I met her, I knew this was true. She's so lovely, she quite took my breath away. Jack must be so proud of her.*

She was shy with me at first, but soon came round and with a wisdom beyond her years, she seemed to accept what I had to tell her. Of course, I can never produce any written proof that Susannah is my daughter, but Jack didn't seem to mind this. He was quite satisfied, especially when I told him my baby had been born on February, 8 1937, which is, of course, Susannah's birthday! I shall stay in England for some time now and get to know both Susannah and Jack better. Susannah told me about the Norwegian girls' visit and the production of The Merchant Of Venice so I shall want to be here to see her perform in that.

Once again, my deepest and warmest thanks. You have made me the happiest woman in the world!

Yours with much love and gratitude, Cecily.

Eileen put the letter down and looked across the table at Louisa, who did not miss the tears shining in her mother's eyes.

'Well,' Eileen began, 'it seems Susannah is related to us, doesn't it? Colin would have been so proud.'

Louisa went and hugged her mother.

'I know, Mum, but we've got to look forward now, not backwards. So much has happened these past few months. We've all been through a great deal of stress, but it's over now. I've got my Michael back and a new cousin and you've got a new niece. We'll have to

ask them all to tea, Mr Priestley, Cecily
and Susannah. A family get-together.
How about at Christmas?'

'I think that's a wonderful idea!'
Eileen cried.

13

The curtains came together for the last time and people were still applauding. The lights in the hall came on and eventually the audience started to break up. Louisa caught snatches of conversation.

'Marvellous! Just like professionals.'

'And so young, especially Portia. She'll go far, that girl.'

'Miss Cayton must be a very proud woman tonight.'

It was the end of the first night's performance of The Merchant Of Venice performed by the girls of Langley Hall. A large hall in the town centre, belonging to the Co-operative Society, had been hired for the week and there would be performances every night until Saturday.

Louisa turned to smile at Cecily and could see that she had been crying. But she looked so happy. On her right sat Jack, grinning like a Cheshire cat. Michael and Eileen were sitting on Louisa's left.

'I wouldn't have missed this for the world,' Cecily breathed and caught hold of Jack's hand.

He squeezed it, smiling at her affectionately.

'My lass, would you believe it?' he said.

On the few rows behind them sat the visiting Norwegian girls, most of them blonde, tall and pretty, chattering away now in their own language, obviously much appreciative of the performance they had just seen. They all spoke good English and had settled in well with their host families. Once the play was over and done with, the Norwegian girls were to give a concert of their own, with singing and dancing, wearing their national costumes.

'We may as well wait here for Susannah,' Louisa said.

They were going back to the house

afterwards, for a small opening night party. Christine Yardley was coming, too, and a couple of Susannah's friends. On Saturday night there would be a bigger party for the whole cast but this was to be held at the school.

Louisa was still mesmerised by Susannah's stunning performance and knew how deeply, too, Cecily and Jack had been affected. Louisa had never seen him look so smart.

The intervening weeks since Cecily's reunion with her daughter had flown by. Another year had started, the spring term now well advanced. Louisa knew that Cecily would be returning to America soon and this would be a sad time for her, but Susannah had come to Louisa a few days ago and said, 'I'm going to America in the summer holidays, Mrs Barton. Dad was a bit doubtful to begin with but now he says I can go.'

The girl was obviously very excited by the prospect. It was amazing how well she had adapted to having a new mother and Louisa could not envisage any undue problems with the sort of transatlantic relationship that would be necessary.

Louisa watched Cecily and Jack now, talking to one another, his head nodding as he listened to what she had to say, occasionally making comments of his own. They were great friends, she could see that. Suddenly life was good. All mysteries solved, all difficulties overcome.

Louisa linked arms with Michael and he smiled at her.

'You were right about Susannah,' he remarked.

'Yes, I know, but Christine was the one who first saw Susannah's potential and she is the one who put in all the hard work with the girls.'

Michael looked around. 'Where is Christine now?' he asked.

'Back stage, I should think. She'll be floating on air for days after tonight.'

And she wouldn't be the only one, Louisa thought with a secret smile. She hadn't said anything to Michael, yet, and she hadn't been to see a doctor, but she was certain she was pregnant and if she was right, she would be having a baby in the autumn.

She would tell Michael tonight.

She turned to see Susannah running across the hall, now changed into her outdoor clothes, eyes bright and shining, looking so happy, so elated. Louisa thought about how Susannah had changed over the months, how life had changed for them all. Now Susannah went first to her father and gave him a fierce hug, before turning to embrace Cecily.

They started to leave the hall, showering compliments on the girl who had so recently stood at the front of a stage for the first time and taken her bows to wild applause. She might follow in her mother's footsteps. She might even become a writer. Who knew?

At the moment, Louisa felt sure, Susannah would only want to continue her studies at Langley Hall. And whatever she decided to do in the future she would always be the same sweet intelligent, thoughtful girl she was now.

Louisa had no doubt of that.

THE END

We do hope that you have enjoyed reading this large print book.

Did you know that all of our titles are available for purchase?

We publish a wide range of high quality large print books including:
Romances, Mysteries, Classics
General Fiction
Non Fiction and Westerns

Special interest titles available in large print are:
The Little Oxford Dictionary
Music Book, Song Book
Hymn Book, Service Book

Also available from us courtesy of Oxford University Press:
Young Readers' Dictionary
(large print edition)
Young Readers' Thesaurus
(large print edition)

For further information or a free brochure, please contact us at:
Ulverscroft Large Print Books Ltd.,
The Green, Bradgate Road, Anstey,
Leicester, LE7 7FU, England.
Tel: (00 44) **0116 236 4325**
Fax: (00 44) **0116 234 0205**

Other titles in the
Linford Romance Library:

VISIONS OF THE HEART

Christine Briscomb

When property developer Connor Grant contracted Natalie Jensen to landscape the grounds of his large country house near Ashley in South Australia, she was ecstatic. But then she discovered he was acquiring — and ripping apart — great swathes of the town. Her own mother's house and the hall where the drama group met were two of his targets. Natalie was desperate to stop Connor's plans — but she also had to fight the powerful attraction flowing between them.